Patrick strode toward her, magnificently bare and completely unashamed.

And that was when it hit her. She was in love with him.

It was quite obvious that he did not love her, yet her heart was his. She had planned a quiet, happy life for herself with some shy, unassuming man. And ended up eloping with one of the Jones boys.

It was crazy. Terrifying. And yet Regina felt absolutely wonderful.

As she had learned yesterday, naked in the sun on Sweetbriar Summit, her life was no longer sane and uneventful. She loved Patrick Jones.

And not only that, she had gone and *married* him.

Dear Reader,

Welcome to Silhouette Special Edition...welcome to romance.

The hot month of July starts off with a sizzling event! Debbie Macomber's fiftieth book, *Baby Blessed*, is our THAT SPECIAL WOMAN! for July. This emotional, heartwarming book in which the promise of a new life reunites a husband and wife is not to be missed!

Christine Rimmer's series THE JONES GANG continues in *Sweetbriar Summit* with sexy Patrick Jones, the second of the rapscallion Jones brothers you'll meet. You'll want to be around when the Jones boys bring their own special brand of trouble to town!

Also this month, look for books by some of your favorite authors: Celeste Hamilton presents us with an emotional tale in *Which Way Is Home?* and Susan Mallery has a *Cowboy Daddy* waiting to find a family. July also offers *Unpredictable* by Patt Bucheister, and *Homeward Bound* by Sierra Rydell, her follow-up to *On Middle Ground*. A veritable light show of July fireworks!

I hope you enjoy this book, and all of the stories to come!

Sincerely,

Tara Gavin
Senior Editor

Please address questions and book requests to:
Silhouette Reader Service
U.S.: 3010 Walden Ave., P.O. Box 1325, Buffalo, NY 14269
Canadian: P.O. Box 609, Fort Erie, Ont. L2A 5X3

CHRISTINE RIMMER

SWEETBRIAR SUMMIT

Silhouette®

SPECIAL EDITION®

Published by Silhouette Books
America's Publisher of Contemporary Romance

In memory of my aunt,
Anna Marie Smith Folsom,
who always fed the children,
was always a lady
and always made room for me at her house.

 SILHOUETTE BOOKS

ISBN 0-373-09896-0

SWEETBRIAR SUMMIT

Copyright © 1994 by Christine Rimmer

Printed in U.S.A.

Books by Christine Rimmer

Silhouette Special Edition

Double Dare #646
Slow Larkin's Revenge #698
Earth Angel #719
Wagered Woman #794
Born Innocent #833
*Man of the Mountain #886
*Sweetbriar Summit #896

*The Jones Gang

Silhouette Desire

No Turning Back #418
Call It Fate #458
Temporary Temptress #602
Hard Luck Lady #640
Midsummer Madness #729
Counterfeit Bride #812

CHRISTINE RIMMER

is a third-generation Californian who came to her profession the long way around. Before settling down to write about the magic of romance, she'd been an actress, a sales clerk, a janitor, a model, a phone sales representative, a teacher, a waitress, a playwright and an office manager. Now that she's finally found work that suits her perfectly, she insists she never had a problem keeping a job—she was merely gaining "life experience" for her future as a novelist. Those who know her best withhold comment when she makes such claims; they are grateful that she's at last found steady work. Christine is grateful, too—not only for the joy she finds in writing, but for what waits when the day's work is through: a man she loves who loves her right back and the privilege of watching their children grow and change day to day.

THE JONES FAMILY TREE

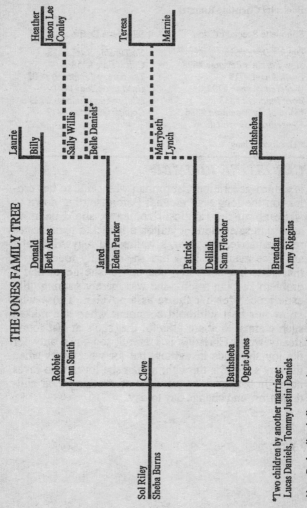

*Two children by another marriage:
Lucas Daniels, Tommy Justin Daniels

Note: Broken lines indicate previous marriage(s).

Chapter One

"You sure you ain't takin' on more than you can handle, son?" Oggie Jones adjusted his suspenders and thoughtfully chewed on his cigar.

"I'm sure." Patrick's tone was utterly flat. He was crouched on his haunches beside the tree where his father sat fishing.

His father was watching him. "Hot damn, you're grim lately."

"It's a grim world sometimes, Dad." Patrick looked out over the river that meandered by about five feet from his boots. Overhead, the fingers of dawn stroked the night sky with growing brightness.

"Well, hell, you never used to be grim. You were always the best-natured one in the family. A player and a charmer."

"Yeah, and look what great things I've done with my life so far." Patrick made no attempt to mask his sarcasm.

Oggie let out one of his rheumy rumbles of laughter. "Well, we all make our mistakes. But you're improvin', you really are. No one would deny that the last few months you've been makin' up for lost time. In spades."

"I want to be ready."

"Just don't give yourself a heart attack."

"Don't worry. I won't."

Oggie reeled in his line and cast it out again. Then he gave his son a sideways glance. "Ain't none of what you've done so far gonna amount to a hill of beans without—"

Patrick knew what was coming next. He put up a hand. "Dad. Don't start."

"What the hell d'you mean, 'don't start'? I ain't *startin'*. You gotta be stopped, to start. I started in about this six months ago, and I've been on it ever since."

"I know."

"And I'm still on it."

"Fine. And you've made your point about it, over and over. There's no need for you to go on about it anymore."

"I'll make you a deal. You tell me what the hell you been doin' about it, and I'll stop goin' on about it."

Patrick sighed. "Dad . . ."

"Go ahead, tell me."

"Damn it."

"That all you've got to say? 'Damn it'? Well, I guess I know what that means. That means you ain't done a thing since the last time we talked, right? You come out here at the crack of dawn, disturbin' the fish, messin' up my peaceful time, to tell me you ain't done squat about your major problem."

"Dad—" Patrick stifled a groan of impatience "—you're the one who left the note on my door to meet you here."

"Damn straight I did. I had to talk to you. I had to find out if you were still draggin' your feet about this. And I was right. You're not just draggin' your feet, boy. You done nailed the both of them clean through the floor."

Patrick shook his head. "Dad, I'm thirty-eight years old."

Oggie snorted and reeled in his line a little, only to let it back out right away. "What's that got to do with anything?"

"A hell of a lot. Ask anyone. They'll tell you that a thirty-eight-year-old man has a right to run his own life."

"Hell, yeah. And you've been runnin' your own life, ain't you? And a lot of good you've done with it so far."

"A minute ago you said we all make our mistakes."

"That was then. This is now." Oggie took his cigar from between his yellowed teeth, flicked off the nonexistent ash and stuck it back into his mouth. "Tell you what I'm gonna do."

"Oh, no."

"I'm gonna let your sarcasm pass."

"That's all? That's what you're gonna do?"

"In your dreams."

"Please," Patrick muttered prayerfully, "let that be all."

"What I'm gonna do, is—"

"Hell."

"Find her *for* you."

Patrick looked at his father for a long time. Then he said, "No, thanks."

"Damn, boy." Oggie chortled. "What're you worried about? My record's good, and you know it."

"I'll find my own woman, Dad."

"You got a lot of requirements for this one. You need some expert assistance."

"The hell I do."

"If you'da taken my help before, you might not be in this mess now."

"I'll say it again. No, Dad."

"What're you worried about? Nobody can force you, anyway. I'll find just what you're lookin' for. You watch. And then, if you don't like her, nobody's gonna chain you to the wall and make you take her." There was more self-satisfied cackling. "You look her over, and you decide for yourself if your old man can't pick 'em."

"This is a disgusting conversation."

"Sometimes a disgusting conversation is what it takes to get the job done."

Patrick straightened and looked down at his father's grizzled head. "I'm going."

Right then, Oggie's line jerked. Oggie sat up and paid attention. "Fine. Get outta here." He began working his reel.

Patrick headed for the short trail that led up to the road. Just as he reached it, Oggie called over his shoulder, "You're movin' tomorrow?"

"You bet."

"I'll be there to help."

"I was afraid you'd say that."

Oggie cackled and let out more line. "You're gonna like her, boy. I can pick 'em. You just wait."

Patrick, pretending he didn't hear his father's last words, continued toward the trail.

By the time he'd reached his 4×4, he'd completely dismissed his father's crazy proposal. Yes, he needed a woman. And his requirements when it came to the woman were very specific. But he'd find her himself when the time came.

Chances were, he'd have to look out of town. He knew every woman in North Magdalene, after all, and he couldn't think of one of them who had the combination of attributes he required.

Yeah, he was going to have to look farther afield, he knew. But right now he couldn't think about where he'd look, let alone when he was going to find the time. He had a full day's work ahead of him, and then he had to go home and finish packing for tomorrow's big move.

No, he wasn't going to worry about finding the right woman until he was moved and settled into the house he'd just bought. Then, one way or another, he'd have to go looking.

Because his father had been right about one thing. Time was running out on him. If he didn't find her soon, everything else he'd done would amount to exactly zero.

Chapter Two

When she heard the shouting, Regina Black was doing just what she always did on Saturday morning after breakfast. She was sitting at her piano practicing the hymns she would play in church the next day.

Before her, the old hymnal lay open on the music desk. Near to hand, a fresh cup of coffee steamed atop a coaster that Regina had crocheted herself.

Regina was playing "In the Garden," a personal favorite of hers. With the hauntingly sweet melody all around her, Regina found it easy to lose herself, to put aside her own insignificant day-to-day troubles. She forgot the loneliness that was often her cross to bear. She slipped the bounds of her own shyness. Her soul soared free.

But then, between one celestial bar and the next, she distinctly heard an elderly sounding man shout outside, "Not that way, you damn fool. Take it left! Left!"

Regina's hands froze above the keys as a woman's voice chimed in, "No, right! You've got to edge it right a little!"

Regina, caught somewhere between the music of the spheres and mundane reality, blinked and stopped playing.

Outside, from the street, the man instructed, "You boys'll have to ease it. Ease it, I say!"

The woman urged, "Be careful, for heaven's sake, or it'll roll right down the street!"

The man shouted, "Great balls of fire! Will you listen to what I'm tellin' ya! Nobody under sixty can be bothered to listen these days. Hell and damnation, I oughtta get up there and do it myself. Why, if I were ten years younger, and not walkin' with this damn cane—"

"Well, you're *not* ten years younger, Dad," another male voice, an exasperated one, pointed out. "Just tell us if we're about to hit anything. Please."

"Well, ain't that what I—"

"Just shut up and tell us."

The voices, Regina decided, were familiar. But that was hardly surprising. Here in the small California town of North Magdalene, where Regina had been born, raised and would no doubt die, the population had not exceeded two hundred and fifty souls since the gold rush. Everybody knew everybody. Sometimes too well.

Regina shrugged. It was none of her business if her neighbors chose to shout at each other on the street. She had her own task before her: the hymns. She drew in a breath, then placed her long, pale hands loosely—wrists neither drooping nor too high—on the keys.

One uplifting chord issued forth.

And then, through her dining room window, she saw a man lurch into view carrying a patio recliner above his head. Regina took off her reading glasses and craned forward to see better. She realized then that the man was one of those wild, unruly Jones boys—the truck driver, Brendan. As Brendan disappeared from her view, his pretty wife, Amy, lugging two folding chairs, appeared and then vanished, as well.

Out on the street, the shouting of commands and complaints, mingled with an occasional burst of laughter, continued. It took no great amount of brainpower to deduce that some branch of the rowdy, larger-than-life Jones clan was moving into the vacant house next door.

Regina, her hymns forgotten, lowered the fall board. Brendan Jones and his wife flashed into view once more, heading back the way they'd come. They were laughing, holding hands.

Regina slid out from behind the piano bench and approached one of the two big windows that flanked her front door. The windows had shades and swag treatments and see-through lace panels. Regina kept the lace panels drawn across the windows all the time. That way she got plenty of light, along with maximum privacy. Plus, she found the lace pretty to look at.

But right now she appreciated the lace for a totally new reason—because she was spying on the Joneses through it. Spying was an activity of which she did not approve. But for some reason, right now, she was doing it anyway.

Regina pondered the notion that a branch of the Jones family would be living next door to her. Her mother, Anthea, would have been outraged at the thought. But Anthea Black had been dead for five years now. She was not here to be outraged.

And Regina wasn't outraged. Not at all. Rather, she was...intrigued. Yes, that was exactly the word. *Intrigued*.

In North Magdalene, after all, the Joneses were the stuff of legend. About forty years ago, old Oggie, who was now standing on the street shouting orders in that cigars-and-whiskey voice of his, had drifted into town out of nowhere, fallen for a local beauty, Bathsheba Riley, and married her within a month of their first meeting. Bathsheba had given him three sons and a daughter.

The sons grew up wild, passionate and bad, each one getting into worse troubles than the last. Two of those three, Jared and Brendan, were married and settled down now, but the stories of their exploits would never die.

The daughter, Delilah, had been the town's most squeaky-pure, upright spinster. For years, she'd avoided the rest of her family the way any good Christian avoids temptation. Why, even Regina's mother had approved of Delilah Jones.

But then a year ago, Delilah had shocked the whole town by running off with, and then marrying, wild Sam Fletcher. And since her marriage, Delilah Jones Fletcher had reunited with her family.

In fact, Delilah was standing on the sidewalk beside her father right this minute, yelling, "I mean it, you've got to edge it right, right!"

It was a huge side-by-side refrigerator. Two men were struggling to maneuver the thing out of the truck and trailer that Brendan owned. Working the dolly together, the two men backed slowly out of the shadows onto the ramp, the hefty appliance above them. Their strong bodies strained forward. They grunted and groaned.

The first man to move into the sunlight was Sam Fletcher. He was a giant of a man, three or four inches taller than the man beside him, with huge muscles that bulged and knotted even under his shirt.

But Regina hardly saw Sam. Her whole consciousness, her entire attention, had been captured and held by the other man.

It was no time at all, from when the other man labored in shadow, and the split second later that he emerged, groaning, into the bright morning light.

It was a very important split second for Regina Black, however, because it was the precise instant when she came to understand that masculine perfection, pure male beauty, had a name: *Patrick Jones.*

Stunned, mesmerized, Regina stared at Oggie Jones's second son. Patrick was not wearing a shirt. The beautiful, perfectly proportioned muscles of his back and shoulders rippled beneath his sweat-shiny skin. He wore khaki-colored jeans and workmen's boots. And a pair of leather work gloves that, somehow, made his naked arms and torso seem all the more bare.

In an unconscious gesture, Regina lifted a hand and placed it over her heart. Why, Patrick Jones was really a very...compelling man.

Suddenly Sam swore and swatted at his neck.

"Whoa, Sam," Patrick warned.

"Damn yellow jacket stung me!" Sam bellowed, as he lost control of his half of the massive load.

Patrick's beautiful muscles leapt and bulged with the strain of taking it all.

On the street, both Oggie and Delilah gasped.

And so did Regina, behind her lace curtain veil.

But then, in a lightning-swift move, Patrick let his side go until it gained the speed of Sam's. Oggie and Delilah shouted and stomped. Then Sam and Patrick, more like dancers than mere moving men, caught up to the load and, groaning, slowed it. It reached the bottom of the ramp and rolled, steady as you please, onto the sidewalk.

Oggie and Delilah, joined by Brendan and Amy, burst into applause. Sam and Patrick, grinning, paused to right the dolly and to bow.

Behind her curtains, Regina smiled.

And then Sam and Patrick laid the refrigerator back on the dolly once more and slowly proceeded up the walk of the vacant house toward the front steps. They passed from Regina's view.

Regina knew only one desire: to keep Patrick Jones in sight. She moved to the side window, near the piano. From there she had a clear view of the neglected, overgrown yard as well as the front porch of the big vacant house. She forgot all about the fact that this particular window had no lace curtains to shield her from the sight of those outside. She was too caught up in watching Patrick, admiring him, gazing in awe and wonder.

He was so alive, so vital. She could see the breath coming in and out of his hard, wide chest. His thick brown hair was longish, falling over his brow and curling at his neck. Regina, hardly knowing what she did, smoothed her own neatly pulled-back hair.

It was so strange. She'd known *of* him all her life. But, of course, she'd never really *known* him. He was only a year or two older than she was and they had been in school at the same time. Yet he was one of those incorrigible Jones boys and she was Anthea Black's shy, sheltered daughter. They had nothing in common. They'd probably never said more than hello to each other three or four times in all of their lives.

It was so odd to see him now. Because, though he'd always been around, she'd never *really* seen him before.

And now she *was* seeing him. And she never wanted to look away.

Her blood moved slow and sweet through her veins. She felt utterly relaxed, her breath sighing gently in and out. Rarely in her proper, carefully prescribed life had she felt quite like this. It frightened her a little, but not enough to make her stop staring.

Until something intruded.

Regina stiffened. She swallowed and licked her lips. Someone was watching her, as she watched Patrick Jones.

Though it was the last thing she wanted to do, she made herself look away from her beautiful discovery, from the masculine perfection that was Patrick Jones. Her dazed glance sought the source of that strange feeling.

And she found herself looking right into the beady eyes of Patrick's father, Oggie Jones.

Regina stared, caught between her own forbidden thoughts and the awareness that she had been found out. The old man must have followed the others halfway up the walk. And then he must have turned.

Slowly Oggie's wizened face crinkled even more as his lips curved into a crafty, knowing smile.

With a sharp cry, Regina leapt back from the window. She retreated to the heart of her large, quiet living room. She sat on the couch, feeling foolish and terribly embarrassed. She shivered, though the day was warm.

Why, the eccentric old coot had grinned at her as if he could see right inside her mind.

Her face flamed. She put her hands to her cheeks to cool them and told herself to settle down, she was being foolish. She'd been caught spying on her neighbors, and she was embarrassed, which she very well ought to be. That was all.

Oggie Jones was an aging eccentric, nothing more. He had no psychic powers. There was no way that Oggie could know for sure what had been going through Regina's mind as she stared at his middle son.

Thank heavens.

And now that she was calmer, her own behavior was beginning to seem distinctly odd.

Regina had no idea what could have gotten into her, to be so utterly mesmerized by the sight of Patrick Jones with his shirt off. The way she'd acted was strange. And she did not approve of it.

Also, she felt just a little bit guilty. As if she'd somehow betrayed Marcus Shelby, who had been her steady date for well over a year now.

Well, she decided, however oddly she'd behaved, she certainly hadn't done anything that terrible. She had snooped and she had . . . entertained erotic thoughts about a man she really hardly knew. But that was all. It was not the end of the world.

Regina stood. She went to her piano. She began to play from Handel's *Messiah*.

With the beautiful music in her ears, her spirit once more soared with the angels.

Unfortunately, the taunting image of a muscled back and sweat-sheened skin still lingered, the way the vision of the sun will stay, burned on the inside of the eyelids, if one is foolish enough to stare directly at it.

Regina refused to let this peculiar phenomenon trouble her. Whatever had happened as a result of looking too long at Patrick Jones would pass; she was sure of it. In a day or two she would have forgotten the incident even occurred.

The next morning she was still in her robe at seven-thirty when the doorbell rang.

Regina assumed it was Nellie Anderson, the church's volunteer secretary, who lived three doors down and across. Nellie was a single lady who had long ago been married, but who'd been widowed for so long, most folks in town had forgotten she'd ever had a husband. She was a terrible gossip. She loved nothing so much as to get on the phone and talk for hours to anyone who wouldn't hang up on her.

Beyond her love for the telephone, Nellie was quite fond of "just dropping in for a minute." She frequently dropped in on Regina at odd hours—such as seven-thirty on Sunday morning.

With a little sigh, Regina straightened her modest cotton robe and went to answer the door. She would offer Nellie one cup of coffee, no more. And she would be frank, though not rude. She hadn't had her breakfast yet, and if Nellie stayed too long, Regina would just have to tactfully mention that she had a million things to accomplish before church this morning.

Since she was sure it was Nellie—though the shades were still drawn and she couldn't see outside—she pasted on a polite smile and opened the door wide.

On her porch stood Patrick Jones.

Chapter Three

Regina emitted a croaky, wispy little sound. It was almost the word *Oh*, but not quite.

Patrick, whose hair was tousled and whose blue eyes drooped lazily as if he'd only just crawled from his bed, gave her a slow smile. "'Morning."

"Er..." She frantically cleared her throat. "Yes. Good morning."

"I'm your new neighbor."

She swallowed. "You are?"

"You bet." He was holding an empty coffee mug in his hand and he gestured with it, offhandedly. "I know you probably heard all the racket yesterday. Look, I'm sorry if we bothered you or anything. Moving in and all, you know. It's a big job."

"Oh. Yes. I'm sure..."

He was wearing pants like the ones from the day before and a faded plaid shirt of soft cotton flannel. The shirt was not buttoned. It took every ounce of determination Regina possessed to keep from staring at the slice of bare chest and hard belly that the open shirt revealed.

She cast her glance downward. And noticed that his feet were bare. They were long, beautifully formed feet, with brown hairs dusting the tops of them. The toenails were clipped short, though not filed smooth.

Suddenly, staring at Patrick Jones's feet, Regina Black wanted to cry.

It was insane, but those feet *moved* her. They were so perfect, so *useful* looking, so strong and yet vulnerable. So clearly a *man's* feet.

Somehow, though it seemed disloyal to Marcus to think such a thing, she could not see herself being moved at the sight of Marcus's feet. Had she ever even *seen* Marcus's feet? She must have, surely. She had known him for nearly two years now. But she couldn't *remember* Marcus's feet. That was the problem.

She could not remember Marcus Shelby's feet. And, at the same time, she was horrifyingly certain that she would never forget the feet of Patrick Jones.

"Regina?"

She lifted her head and made herself look into those blue, blue eyes. "What?"

"Are you all right?"

"Um . . . yes. Fine. Perfectly fine."

He smiled again, this time somewhat ruefully. "I know it's early. But my dad just showed up." He gestured over his shoulder.

Out on the street, the ancient, rather rusty Cadillac Eldorado that Oggie Jones had owned ever since Regina could remember, sat parked between a compact car and a minivan.

"I see," Regina mumbled inanely.

"The point is, he won't go away until he gets coffee. And he won't drink coffee unless it's loaded with sugar. And I don't have any sugar."

"You want to borrow some sugar."

"Exactly."

"Oh. Well, sure."

"Great."

Again he held up the coffee mug he'd brought with him. Regina looked at it for a moment, wondering what it was for.

And then she remembered. The sugar.

"Oh. Yes. Of course."

Praying that her face wasn't as red as it felt, she took the cup from him and turned for the kitchen, so flustered by the confused tumble of feelings he inspired in her, that she didn't even realize she'd left him standing there at the door without so much as a "be right back."

In her old-fashioned kitchen with its tall wooden cabinets, she had to reach high to bring down the sugar canister. And then she almost dropped the blasted thing before getting it safely to the counter, because she saw from the corner of her eye that Patrick had followed her into the house.

"Nice house." He lounged in the doorway to the hall, watching her in a way that made her more nervous by the second. "I've always liked old houses. That's one of the reasons I took the one next door. Plus, those two ladies from Oakland who owned it made some nice improvements to it. Like adding central air. And then, they were in a hurry to sell—and get back to the big city, I guess. So I also got quite a deal."

Regina didn't reply. She concentrated on scooping the sugar into the cup, capping the canister and putting it away.

Though she wasn't looking at him, it seemed to her she could feel his gaze, and she shivered a little, because she sensed then that he really was watching her very closely. When she rose on tiptoe to return the canister to its shelf, she was overly conscious of the way the fabric of her robe molded her breasts.

"This house of yours is a big house for one person, though," he went on, in a musing tone.

She turned to him, holding his cup of sugar close to her body. "I grew up in this house." She felt, suddenly, defiant. She wasn't even aware that her shyness had fallen away.

"I know. You used to be sick all the time, as a kid, weren't you?"

She looked at him, not answering. It was a sensitive subject for her. Now that her mother was dead and Regina's own personality was at last asserting itself, she had begun to understand that her endless chain of childhood ills had probably not been nearly as serious as her mother had always made them seem. Regina realized now that her mother, widowed at a young age, had been extremely possessive. It had suited Anthea Black to have a sickly daughter. That way she could keep her only child home more and close to her side, not to mention under her strict control.

Regina's silence seemed to worry Patrick. "Was that out of line, or something, to ask you that?"

"No." Disarmed by his concern for her feelings, she relaxed a little. "Really. It's okay. And you're right. I was a sickly child." She lifted her chin. "But I'm quite healthy now."

He grinned at that, and then shrugged. "This is North Magdalene, what can I say? We all know it all, don't we? About each other." And then he started walking toward her.

Regina's whole body tightened. Her eyes widened. His skin gleamed at her between the open plackets of his shirt.

His step as he approached was utterly masculine, strong and sure and direct.

And Regina, mesmerized by the sight of Patrick coming ever closer, found herself suddenly flung back in time to a certain morning during her childhood, the morning she came face-to-face with a mountain lion....

It had been a Sunday, like today, a Sunday before church. She'd been wearing her blue dotted swiss dress with the sailor collar and her little patent leather Mary Janes. It had been during one of her "well times," between one illness and the next.

Since for once she seemed to be neither flushed nor congested, her mother had allowed her to go out in the yard for a moment before they left for Sunday service. As children will, she had wandered through the gate and down to the end of the street where the woods began, into the cool shadows of the trees.

And the mountain lion had been waiting there, in the arms of a giant oak. She was instantly aware of it, because everything was suddenly silent, all the other animals nearby either fled or hiding. She looked slowly around her until she saw it, there in the tree, staring at her, still and watchful.

She was five years old, and frail. Easy prey.

The mountain lion laid its ears flat and granted her a low, hissing snarl. Slowly she began to back up, out of the darkness of the trees and into the sunlight at the end of her street. The mountain lion held her gaze, but didn't move.

Just as she felt the welcome sun on her back, she heard her mother calling. "Regina! Regina, where have you gone off to?"

She whirled and ran, the muscles in her back twitching, expecting any second to feel the leaping weight of the cat, the hard dig of its claws, tearing dotted swiss and tender flesh.

But it didn't happen. She ran to her mother's arms.

And when her mother asked what was wrong, she only held on and whispered, "Nothing, Mama. Nothing, honest."

Regina had known what would happen if she told. Her mother would have seen that the mountain lion was shot. And Regina, child of the mountains, knew that to shoot the big cat before it actually attacked someone would probably be the best thing.

Yet she had never told anyone about it. Perhaps she had looked too long into its eyes....

Regina blinked. Patrick Jones was standing in front of her. She gave him the sugar. As he took the mug, one side of one finger brushed her hand. She had to suppress a startled gasp at the little, heated shock that skittered up her arm from just that brushing touch.

"Thanks."

Her shyness, which had been for a short time blessedly suspended, came crashing in on her. "Sure. Um ... anytime."

She felt like a complete idiot. Always, Regina had been shy around strong, self-assured individuals. And, with this man right now, her shyness seemed ten times worse than usual.

They stared at each other.

Oh, this simply could not go on. She simply had to put this—whatever it was he did to her senses—aside. That was all there was to it.

He was only her neighbor, here to borrow sugar as neighbors often did. She had to stop quivering and thinking of mountain lions whenever she looked at him.

She forced herself to ask a neighborly question. "Are you, um, getting settled in all right?"

Patrick smiled again. "Well enough. It's a big job, but the family's helping."

"Well, that's nice." She winced at how asinine she sounded, but at least she was talking about normal, everyday things. She remembered his veiled dig about how big her house was, and she gave it right back to him. "That's a big house, isn't it? For a man alone."

He chuckled, and then grew serious. "Yeah. It's exactly what I need. I have to have the extra rooms for when my girls come home."

Regina stared blankly at him for a moment, before she remembered that last year the word around town was that Marybeth, his ex-wife, had taken his two daughters and moved to Arkansas. She nodded. "Ah. I see. When your daughters visit, you want them to have plenty of room."

"Right. There's a bedroom for Teresa and one for Marnie, too."

"Yes. Of course. That's good."

"It's necessary." His voice was gruff, his eyes hooded. Regina had no idea what he might be thinking. He seemed to shake himself. "Well. Gotta go."

"Yes. Of course."

He turned for the front door. She followed, feeling like a leaf blown in the wake of a forceful wind.

At the door, just before he went out, she made herself offer, like a good neighbor should, "Um ... Patrick ... if there's anything at all I can do to help you get settled in, then you let me know. I mean it. Okay?"

He turned and those sapphire eyes seemed to bore right through her. Then that beautiful smile returned. "Yeah. Thanks, Regina. You're great."

And he was gone.

Regina couldn't help herself. Like some giddy schoolgirl, she leaned against the door and sighed.

And then she straightened and spoke firmly to herself. She told herself that, from now on, all this flighty foolishness would cease.

Patrick Jones was a thoroughly unsuitable man for a woman like herself. First of all, there was the fact that a rather prim, introverted person like herself could surely hold no attraction for a virile, rugged man like he was. And second, charming as he was, Patrick Jones had a very poor record when it came to relationships with women.

A woman would have to be asking for trouble to so much as *consider* getting involved with him, no matter how beautiful his smile or how stunning his male form. And besides that, there was Marcus, with whom she was developing a lovely, warm, meaningful relationship. Regina intended to marry Marcus, though Marcus had yet to speak to her of marriage.

But that would come, Regina was certain. One day soon, Marcus Shelby would propose. Regina would say yes. Instead of the one *playing* "The Wedding March," Regina would be the one walking down the aisle to it. She and Marcus would settle into a contented life. Perhaps they would even be blessed with a child or two.

Patrick Jones, on the other hand, was her neighbor and nothing more. From now on she would treat him as such.

Chapter Four

"Here's your damn sugar."

"Thanks, son." Oggie sat with his feet on one of Patrick's kitchen chairs, puffing on a fat cigar. "That was downright obligin' of you, to consider my sweet tooth like that." He actually sounded grateful.

Patrick should have been warned. When Oggie Jones sounded grateful, it was only to throw a man off his guard. Patrick plunked the sugar on the table beside his father's coffee cup—and failed to pull his hand away fast enough.

The old man's knotted fingers closed around his wrist. "Look me in the eye."

"You old coot."

"I mean it. Look at me."

Reluctantly, Patrick did as his father instructed.

Oggie peered at Patrick for a moment, and then chortled in a kind of triumphant glee. "Yeah. I'm right, ain't I? She's the one."

Patrick yanked his arm free and glared down at his father. "You had to have that damn sugar. Use it."

The old man chortled some more as he poured about half the sugar Regina Black had given Patrick into his cup.

"What the hell is so damn funny?"

"Life, son. Life." Oggie picked up a butter knife, since no spoon was handy in the chaos of Patrick's half-unpacked kitchen. He stirred his coffee with the knife. "She's kinda pretty, ain't she? In a low-key kind of way."

"Who?"

"You know damn well who." The old man sipped from the cup. "She always appealed to me, personally. With those big gray eyes and that soft pale skin. She's a woman you gotta look close at. But when you do, you get that feelin', you know what I mean? That there's more to her than, um, meets the eye. . . ."

"Don't push it, Dad," Patrick warned in a quiet voice. Then he went to the counter and began plowing through an open packing box looking for another mug.

Oggie Jones shrugged, sipped again from his coffee-flavored cup of sugar, and kept talking. "But she had that dragon of a mother around all the time until a few years ago. For too long it looked like no man would ever have her. A real loss to the male population of our fair town, I gotta say. A woman like that's a prize. She's stable and steady. You can see she's born to be a wife. And yet, you look close, you watch the way she'll finger the keys of a piano when she plays, you know she's got real potential, er, between the sheets."

"I don't really need to hear this, Dad," Patrick said as he poured some coffee.

"Sure you do. Where was I? Oh, right. And now the mother's gone. And your only competition's that wimpy twit that runs the grocery store." Oggie leaned back, lifting the front feet of his chair off the floor. "Yessiree. Who woulda thought it, you and sweet little Regina Black?" The smelly cigar was brandished grandly. "Hell, son. Ain't no use you fightin' it. She's exactly what you're lookin' for. And beyond that, judgin' by the way she was spyin' on you yesterday, she's done picked you out as the focus of her, er, secret passions."

Patrick turned, leaned against the counter and took a sip from his cup. "She's scared to death of me."

Oggie was significantly silent. For a moment. Then, "So I ain't gonna have to chain you to the wall to make you take her?"

"Very funny."

"You'll take her. Admit it."

"Like I said, she's scared to death of me."

"So? Go easy." Oggie chortled some more. "But not too easy. You ain't a man who can afford to waste any time over this."

"I know what I have to do, Dad."

"Act real casual, no more than neighborly, for a while."

"I know, Dad."

"But not forever. The time will come, and it won't be too long. You'll have to make your move."

"Dad, I know."

"Good. So go easy, she's a tender thing. But get it handled, get it done...."

After church, Marcus walked Regina home.

She was pleased when he took her hand in his. She was also quite proud of herself that not once did she compare Marcus's pale, rather colorless eyes to clear blue ones, or his nervous grin to a certain easy smile.

When they reached her front gate, she just happened to notice that Patrick was out mowing the overgrown lawn at his new house. He looked up and saw them and waved in a manner that Regina decided was quite suitable.

It was a neighborly wave, friendly but completely offhand. Marcus remarked sourly that the fellow really ought to wear a shirt.

Regina, who was not the least concerned about her neighbor's bare chest, merely shrugged and asked Marcus in for lunch.

Two days later, to Regina's surprise, Patrick knocked on her door at eight in the morning and held up a lovely string of trout.

"Dad and I went fishing. Since he's retired, he's always got a line in the water. My freezer's full, and I thought maybe..."

Regina, who was very glad that she was dressed for the day this time, dared an appreciative—yet no wider than appropriate smile. "Why, thank you, Patrick. That's quite neighborly of you."

"Hey, you're doing *me* the favor. I hate to see them go to waste." He handed over the fish.

"Why, you've cleaned them and everything."

"Yeah. I was doing the others, so I thought I might as well get the whole disgusting job out of the way."

"Well, that's just really—"

His smile changed for a moment. "Neighborly. Right?"

She wondered if he was being sarcastic. But then she decided not to wonder too hard.

"Yes," she said, and kept her smile.

"Well, then. Enjoy."

"I will. Thanks again."

She stood on her porch and gazed after him as he jumped the fence to his side. Then she went in and cooked two of the fish for her breakfast, before heading over to old Mrs. Leslie's to help her clean her house.

That Saturday, in the afternoon, Regina walked over to the church carrying a splendid bouquet of lilies and amaryllis fresh from her garden to adorn the altar for services the next day. She had no sooner returned home than she heard pounding noises coming from next door.

She glanced out a window to see Patrick on his porch, down on his hands and knees. He was wielding a hammer with great concentration. As usual, he wore no shirt, but Regina did not pause for even an extra second to stare.

A half hour later, the pounding was still going on, interspersed with the sounds of a power saw's whine from down in his basement. The day was quite warm. Perhaps Patrick had grown thirsty. Carpentry, in Regina's experience, was thirst-causing work. And he had been so thoughtful, bringing her those lovely fish the other day.

She was out the door with an icy glass of lemonade in her hand before she even stopped to think twice. She strode around through the front gate, and marched up to the base of his porch steps.

He stopped his hammering and sat back on his knees. "Hi, Regina." He wiped his forehead with the back of his leather glove. She caught a quick glimpse of the matted hair beneath his muscled arm, before forcing her gaze to stay on his sweating, flushed face.

She held out the lemonade. "I thought you might appreciate this about now." She was proud of how cordial, how nonchalant, she sounded.

He took off his right glove. "Whew. Thanks." Then he reached for the glass with his ungloved hand and drank long and deep. She tried not to watch his strong throat move as he swallowed, or to notice the sweat that dripped down his neck and onto his bare, sculpted chest, where it caught in the shiny brown hairs there.

He finished the glass and handed it back.

"Would you like some more?"

"Naw. That was just right."

She looked at the porch. "Repairs?"

"Yeah. Some of these porch boards were rotted, and some are loose." He gestured at the place he'd been hammering. Then he winked at her. "Can't have that."

"Oh, absolutely not."

"What with the garage and helping out with the Mercantile Grill, I haven't had a lot of spare time. But little by little, I'm getting this place in shape." Several months ago he'd taken over the town service station. But Regina hadn't heard that he was involved with North Magdalene's newest restaurant.

Regina remarked, "So you're in on the Mercantile Grill, too?"

"Yeah. The Mercantile building itself is sort of my inheritance, from Dad, you know?"

"I think I did hear that somewhere."

The landmark building Patrick referred to was next door to the local tavern, the Hole in the Wall. For over forty years, Oggie Jones had been the proprietor of the Hole in the Wall. But last year, the old man had finally retired. Now Patrick's brother, Jared, and Jared's wife, Eden, managed the bar, as well as their new restaurant.

"Let's face it," Patrick said. "It's really Eden who's running things. She's the business genius in the family. But I'm a partner. I helped with the construction of the interior. And I pitch in whenever they're shorthanded."

"I haven't eaten there yet, but I hear it's very good."

Patrick's gaze shifted suddenly. He was looking at something over her shoulder. "You've got company."

Regina turned to see the tall, reed-thin figure of Nellie Anderson standing at her front gate. Nellie called, "Regina, there you are."

Even from several yards away, that look of sharp interest was clear on Nellie's pinched face. Regina kept her chin high, reminding herself that Patrick was her neighbor and she was being neighborly and if Nellie wanted to make something of that, it was Nellie who had a problem.

Nellie was already at Patrick's gate. She came through and strode up the walk, her long nose in the air. Her small, piercing eyes made a disapproving sweep over Patrick's bare chest. "Hello, Patrick. I hope you're getting settled in well enough."

"Just fine," Patrick said. "Thank you."

Nellie looked at Regina. "The pastor's changed a few of the songs for tomorrow. I thought I'd just drop the list by."

"Fine. Let's go on over to my house." Regina started to usher Nellie toward the gate.

But Nellie spoke again before Regina could lead her away. "Patrick, do you hear anything from Chloe?"

Patrick looked at Nellie for a moment; it was an unreadable kind of look. Then he answered, "No, not a thing." Regina felt a little stab of sympathy for him. She imagined he must have grown very tired of being asked that question over the past several months since Chloe Swan, an old flame of his, had run off with a stranger.

"Chloe's mother, as I'm sure you know, is devastated." Nellie spoke as if Chloe Swan's behavior were Patrick's personal responsibility.

"So?" Patrick's expression remained as carefully bland as his tone.

Regina's sympathy for him increased. In some ways, it must be quite a challenge to lead the kind of life he'd led, to have the town gossips always panting after the next juicy tidbit concerning one's affairs.

"It's a terrible shame, that's all," Nellie intoned.

"Is it?" Now Patrick looked bored. "She's been gone for more than a year now. Maybe she's happy, wherever she is."

"How can you say that?"

"Because it's damn likely to be true."

Nellie gave a small snort of disgust. "Well, it appears that it suits *you* to think so."

Regina had heard enough. She firmly took the older woman's elbow. "Nellie, let's leave Patrick to his work. Come over to my house. I've just made lemonade."

Nellie turned her indignant expression on Regina. "I say what's on my mind, Regina. There's no sense in trying to stop me."

"Ain't that the truth," Patrick muttered.

Nellie's head snapped around. "What was that?"

Regina pulled Nellie away. "He was only agreeing with you, that's all. Now please let's go."

Nellie emitted a pained sigh, but allowed herself to be led off. "Fresh lemonade, you said?"

"I did."

"Good, then. I'm parched."

"See you ladies later," Patrick called, too pleasantly, from behind them. Regina waved without turning—and kept a firm hold on Nellie's bony arm.

Once inside the house, Regina was subjected to a spirited harangue concerning the sins of all the Joneses, Patrick in particular. A single sip from her glass of lemonade and Nellie was off and ranting.

"I tell you, they're all alike, all of them, those Joneses, I swear. Except for our dear Delilah, of course." Nellie and Delilah had been good friends for years. "And Patrick is the worst of them. Do you know that while he was in high school, they used to call him "Love 'em and leave 'em" Jones, because it was just one innocent girl after another for him back then.

"And then, in his twenties, marrying Marybeth Lynch because we all knew he *had* to, even though everyone was certain he loved Chloe Swan. And next, compounding his error by getting Marybeth pregnant a second time, before that poor woman finally got smart and divorced him.

"And, four years ago when Marybeth was out of the picture, did he marry Chloe—poor child, still in love with him—and settle down with her as we all knew he should? No. He continued to *insist,* as he had all through his marriage, that he and Chloe were no more than friends. Until Chloe became so desperate, she took off with a stranger."

Nellie paused to refresh herself with another sip of lemonade. But she was far from finished. "And what of those poor little girls of Patrick's? Not only products of a broken home, but now dragged away from all their friends and loved ones, off to Arkansas with that flighty mother of theirs? It is a crying shame, I tell you, Regina. A crying shame."

Regina, who should have known better than to argue with Nellie Anderson, found she couldn't keep quiet any longer.

"I believe," she ventured, "that Patrick bought the house next door at least partly so he'd have a place for his daughters, during their visits."

"That's what he told *you,* I'm sure."

"Yes, and he seemed very sincere about needing a house with plenty of room in it for his children. And I understand he's settled down lately, that he's doing quite well running the garage and all. And I have to say, he's a model neighbor. Quiet and pleasant and no trouble to have around."

Regina fell silent as she realized that Nellie's nose actually seemed to be twitching, the way a house cat's nose will twitch at the sight of a plump little mouse. "My sweet heavens, Regina. You must never believe anything a man like that tries to tell you."

"All I'm saying, Nellie, is that people do change. They learn and they grow."

Nellie let out a long, discouraged breath. She shook her head sadly. "Oh, Regina, Regina. What is happening to you? I knew it, the moment I saw you talking to him. I sensed what was happening."

"Nothing is happening."

"Oh, my, such an innocent you are. He's a *Jones,* Regina. You haven't a prayer of saving yourself, if you get involved with a man like that."

"I'm not getting involved with him."

"You say that, but what do you know? You've led such a sheltered life. You know nothing of the ways of men like him. Why, remember our poor Delilah, determined for all those years never to so much as get near a man like her father and brothers. And then Sam Fletcher, who we all know is more Joneslike than the Joneses themselves, decided he wanted her. And he stopped at nothing to have her. You remember. This whole town remembers. And the poor girl simply hadn't a prayer. Now she's bound to him for the rest of her life."

"Delilah loves Sam," Regina dared to point out.

"Well, certainly she loves him. That's what I'm saying. She loves him, and now she'll never escape him."

"But that's the point. She doesn't *want* to escape him."

"Exactly. It's a tragedy, a tragedy, plain and simple. And you are so much like her, Regina. A good girl, a nice girl..."

Regina stood. "Nellie. I am not a girl. I am thirty-six years old. I qualify as a full-grown woman, and I *will* be treated as such. And I must tell you, I resent your inference in this instance."

"You—"

"Yes, I do. I resent it." Regina's face felt like it was on fire, and she couldn't believe her own boldness, talking right back to Nellie Anderson like this. But she couldn't, *wouldn't* allow Nellie to assume things that were not in the very least bit true. "You know that I am...seriously involved with Marcus Shelby. I have no interest whatsoever in any other man, and certainly not in Patrick Jones. So I would appreciate it if you would stop this foolishness right now. Patrick Jones and I have nothing in common. Our only connection is that we are neighbors. And that will remain our only connection. Have I made myself clear?"

Nellie's mouth was hanging open. She snapped it closed. Then she meekly allowed, "Well, certainly. If you say so, dear."

"I do say so. I most certainly do."

There was a long and quite uncomfortable silence. Then Nellie drank from her lemonade again. "That was so refreshing." Her voice was cautiously bright. "Could I trouble you for one more glass, do you think?"

"Why, of course, Nellie."

"You are so kind."

Regina refilled Nellie's glass, and her own.

"Thank you."

"You're welcome."

"Here is the list of changes for the hymns for tomorrow."

"Fine."

"And you know, dear, I was wondering, would you be willing to coordinate a few things for the Independence Day picnic this year? The pastor has asked me to get my committee heads in order right away."

"Of course I'll help out wherever I'm needed."

"I knew you'd say that. You are such a thoughtful gir...er woman, dear."

Regina suppressed her small smile of triumph and drank her lemonade.

For the next week, Regina hardly saw her new neighbor. She assumed he was busy at the garage. And she kept busy, too.

Though Regina's mother had left her well provided for, and she didn't really have to work, she enjoyed giving her services to those in need. She helped out with the elderly and with local shut-ins, cooking and cleaning and doing whatever needed to be done. During the school term, she also worked part-time for the North Magdalene School as the secretary/receptionist, a job that she thoroughly enjoyed. And she was always available to give her time to community projects. She led a quite productive life, actually.

And, also, there was Marcus. He really was such a gentle, good man. Saturday night, he took her to the Mercantile Grill for dinner.

Regina had a wonderful time. The service was good and the food even better. She chatted briefly with Eden Jones, congratulating her on her accomplishment with the restaurant—and expressing good wishes for the baby Eden was due to deliver in the fall. Eden, as always, was gracious and warm. She mentioned how much work Patrick had done on the design and construction of the interior. Regina agreed it looked terrific.

When Marcus took Regina home, he came in for coffee. He kissed her, a brief brush of his lips on hers, as he was leaving. Regina stood in her doorway for a moment after he was gone, staring out at the warm summer night, full of vague yearnings that she refused to examine too closely.

Just before she pulled the door closed, she noticed the moths, throwing themselves against the porch light. And she thought that she could understand them, risking everything to reach the burning globe that drew them.

But then she told herself she was being foolish. She was richly blessed, really. She led a useful, meaningful life. She was not and never would be a moth drawn to a flame.

That Tuesday night, she was sitting on her porch swing just after dusk, idly rocking back and forth when her neighbor spoke to her.

"Nice night, huh?" He was leaning on the low wrought-iron fence between their houses.

Her pulse quickened. She ignored the sensation. "Yes, it is."

She didn't invite Patrick to join her, but still he jumped the fence and came and sat on the porch with her. For a moment, she considered asking that he leave. But he didn't even come that close to her. He perched on the porch railing and looked up at the brightening stars.

They talked idly, of nothing important. And in a few moments, he was gone.

It seemed to Regina a thoroughly harmless incident, which was why, when it happened twice more over the next two weeks, she thought little of it. He was her neighbor, and now and then he would join her for a few minutes, at twilight, to watch the stars grow vivid in the darkening sky.

And, of course, she was not thinking of her neighbor at all when, on the last Friday in June, Marcus called early in the morning.

He sounded very nervous, and said he had something important to discuss with her. Would she come to his house tonight at seven for dinner? They could talk afterward.

Regina's heart grew light. She knew, at last, that Marcus Shelby was going to propose.

* * *

"More coffee, Regina?" Marcus asked. Regina noticed that his narrow face was slightly flushed, though the room was not overly warm.

She felt a little shiver of anticipation. Their dinner was finished and cleared away. The moment when he would speak of that important something was upon them.

"No, thank you, Marcus. Two cups are my limit."

There was a silence. Regina smiled at Marcus. Marcus smiled in return.

"Well," Marcus said at last, tucking his napkin beside his dessert plate and then blowing out the candles in the center of the table. "Shall we move into the other room?"

Regina stood. "That sounds lovely."

They went into Marcus's large living room and sat on either end of the wide, comfortable couch. Regina canted toward Marcus and laid an arm along the backrest. Marcus, looking very nervous, sat straight and faced squarely forward.

Regina felt great tenderness toward him at that moment. How difficult it must be to be a man. To be the one expected to do the pursuing, the inviting . . . and the proposing.

"Regina, as I mentioned on the phone this morning," Marcus began, "I have something I must talk with you about."

"Yes, Marcus."

"It is my hope, my fondest wish . . . Oh, how can I put this?"

She waited, knowing this was something he must do in his own way and time.

"Regina, what I'd like to say first, is that I sincerely hope you will not take offense at what I have to say."

Regina frowned a little. How could she possibly take offense at a marriage proposal? "Marcus, I—"

"Please. This is difficult."

"Well, of course, I understand. I do."

He turned toward her then, and his face looked congested, so high was his color. "I hope so."

She was concerned for him suddenly. He truly did look distressed. "Marcus? What is it? You must tell me, whatever it is."

He drew in a long breath. "Regina . . ."

"Yes. What? Say it, please, Marcus."

"Regina, people are talking."

She stared at him. "People are what?"

Suddenly it seemed too much for him to remain seated. He jumped to his feet and walked to the window that looked out on his street. He stuck his hands in his pockets, drew his rather narrow shoulders up and then he faced her once more. "Yes." His tone was grim—and just a bit accusatory. "People are talking about you and Patrick Jones."

Regina simply gaped. It took several moments for her mind to absorb what he was saying. It was very far from what she'd hoped to hear. But then she did absorb it.

And she didn't like it one bit. She withdrew her arm from the back of the couch and folded her hands primly in her lap. "And just what, precisely, are people saying?"

Marcus raked his fingers back through his fine, pale hair. "You *are* offended. I knew you would be."

"What are they saying, Marcus?"

"Regina . . ."

"If this is bothering you, Marcus, then we've got to talk about it frankly. We must have it all right out in the open so that we can see what we're dealing with."

"Well, I know, but . . ."

"But what?"

"Well . . . you're angry. You know how I feel about anger."

Now it was Regina's turn to draw in a long breath. She reminded herself that Marcus was very sensitive. Displays of strong emotion distressed him. It was one of the things the two of them had in common—or so she'd always told herself.

"Yes," she admitted after a moment. "I'm angry—but I'm settling down now."

"Good." Marcus looked massively relieved.

Regina took several more long breaths. And then, when she felt calmer, she patted the couch beside her. "Come. Sit down. Tell me everything, please."

His expression reluctant, he approached and sat down once more at his end of the couch. "Well, Nellie Anderson said she found you in Patrick Jones's yard Saturday before last. And more than one person has seen him, sitting on your porch, in the evenings."

Regina felt her anger—a defensive anger—stirring again, but she immediately quelled it. She wondered vaguely what was happening to her lately. She had actually argued with Nellie Anderson, and now she'd become angry at the idea of people gossiping about herself and Patrick Jones. Arguing and becoming angry as a reaction to other people's behavior were very unlike her. She was a peacemaker by nature, and she rarely got mad.

She spoke slowly and softly. "Marcus, Patrick Jones is my neighbor. No more, no less. He brought me some trout, and I repaid his kindness by offering him a glass of lemonade on that day Nellie's talking about. Once or twice, he's come over to say hello in the evenings. But that is all. If people are talking, it's only because they have vivid imaginations. There is nothing whatsoever between Patrick Jones and me, and there never will be."

"Are you sure?" Marcus, whose head had been bowed as she spoke, looked up. She saw how he wanted to believe her.

"Positive."

"Oh, Regina. You know what they say about the Jones men. They're hopelessly overbearing and disorderly and crude. But once one of them decides to pursue a woman, he always wins her in the end."

"It's only what people say, Marcus. It's gossip. That's all."

"But from what I understand, it's also true."

"Marcus. Patrick Jones has no interest in me whatsoever, I'm sure of it. And if he had, it wouldn't matter. I have no interest in him." *If I do, I'll never pursue that interest,* she guiltily amended to herself. Then she concluded on a plaintive note, "Please believe me. I'm telling you the truth."

Marcus studied her intently for a moment. And then, at last, he smiled. "I am just so pleased to hear that."

Regina, who hadn't realized how tightly she was holding herself, felt her body relax. "Good. Now can we put this nonsense behind us?"

He took her hand. "Absolutely."

"Well, that's a relief." She managed a weak chuckle.

Marcus's pale eyes were very soft. "You know, Regina, I would have been devastated if you'd told me there actually was something between you and Patrick Jones. I have... such very special feelings for you myself."

Regina felt chastened. Marcus *did* care for her. And deeply, too. He was just shy, and sensitive, as she was. She mustn't rush him. The day when he asked her to marry him would come yet. And on that day, she was sure, all of these distressing desires of hers that seemed to center around Patrick Jones would fade away to nothing at all.

Chapter Five

The next week was a busy one for Regina. Besides all the usual tasks she set for herself, she had taken on a lot of the preparatory work for the community church's annual Independence Day Picnic and Bazaar, which was coming up on Saturday, the third of July.

To Regina, it seemed as if she never had a spare moment that whole week.

She spent hours on the phone, arranging for the hundred and one things that had to be delivered to the picnic site on Saturday morning.

There were folding tables and chairs, big commercial barbecues and bag after bag of charcoal briquettes. There were huge tubs in which the soft drinks would be set out, along with hundreds of pounds of party ice. She'd also agreed to coordinate the potluck, which meant she had to contact just about everyone in town and badger them until they agreed to come through with a dessert or a side dish.

Beyond that, in a particularly weak moment, she'd somehow managed to volunteer to bake twenty dozen cookies herself. So her entire Thursday and most of Friday would be given over to standing by the oven, waiting for the timer to ring so she could pull out the next batch.

This year, the picnic was to be held in Sweetbriar Park, a lovely wooded area right across the river from town. And it promised to be a bigger event than on any previous year. The town merchants, including Marcus, were all making major donations of food and goods. Also, Delilah Fletcher, for years the only churchgoing member of the Jones family, had decided it was high time the rest of the Jones clan helped out. Therefore, both Amy and Eden had shown up at all the planning meetings over the past few weeks.

Eden, who'd worked most of her life in restaurants and clubs, had several wonderful ideas for events. So this year, thanks to Eden's suggestions, the picnic would include a raffle, a treasure hunt and after dark, dancing beneath the stars.

Throughout the week, as she raced around trying to get everything done, Regina made it a point to scrupulously avoid her handsome next-door neighbor. Marcus was the man for her, after all. And she didn't want him hearing any more town gossip about herself and the other man, no matter how unfounded that gossip might be.

So on Tuesday night, when Patrick waved to her as she stole a few moments out on her porch, she only returned his wave in a perfunctory manner and went right inside, so he'd have no chance to join her.

Then on Thursday, early in the morning, as she hurried over to Marcus's store to buy more of the margarine she needed to bake all those cookies, she saw Patrick leaving his house.

"Hey, wait up. I'll walk with you!" he called.

But she only waved back, pretending not to hear him, and got in her car to drive the short distance to Main Street. She was taking no chances that he might catch up with her on the way.

It was strange, but now that she had consciously decided to avoid him, she did feel that he sometimes seemed to be watching her, studying her, as if he were *waiting* for something....

But that was ridiculous, she knew. She only imagined he was watching her. It was all in her mind.

A forceful, elemental man such as Patrick could never look at Regina the way a man looks at a woman he desires. He had dated the most attractive girls in the county and married the lovely Marybeth Lynch. Though he'd denied it for years now, everyone knew he'd once been in love with Chloe Swan, who was blond, outgoing, generously proportioned and very, very beautiful. He was not going to suddenly decide he couldn't live without diffident, mousy-haired Regina Black.

Regina firmly told herself that Patrick Jones was not the least bit interested in her. And the notion that he might actually be pursuing her was utterly absurd.

"All right, what the hell's goin' on?" Oggie demanded to know.

Patrick was alone with his father in the back room of the Hole in the Wall. Patrick sipped from his long-neck bottle of beer and stared at his boots, which were crossed at the ankles on the felt-topped table in front of him.

"She's dodging me every chance she gets. Old lady Anderson caught her bringing me lemonade a while back. I guess the old bat started talking and Regina decided she'd better keep away from me."

"Nellie Anderson is always talkin'. You should have allowed for that."

Patrick granted his father a flat look. "I'm doing the best I can, Dad."

"Do better. You gotta see your goal, and never let go of it. Like me and your sainted mother, bless her sweet, sweet soul. After I bought this place and got down on my knees to her and she told me yes, I thought I had everything. But Rory Drury was still after her. And he was a cutthroat son-ofabitch."

"Dad, I've heard this be—"

"Don't interrupt. Your mama taught you better than that."

"Hell, Dad."

"Where was I? Oh. Yeah." Though he winced at the pain in his joints when he did it, Oggie hoisted his own feet up on the table across from his son's. "Rory Drury wasn't a man to give in easy. And so he went and set me up, damned if he didn't. Robbed his own father's safe and took his mama's pearls and diamonds. And planted 'em at my place. Then he sent Davey Bowles—he was sheriff in those days—to bring me in. They took me off to the jail, arraigned me and gave me my grand jury hearing, all without bail. It was a setup, 'cause them Drurys were big people in these parts back then."

"Dad..."

"But I got out of it, didn't I? I got your mama to go to Rory and sweet-talk him until he told her what he'd done. She got it all on tape, too. And if you think that wasn't a damn achievement, you don't know squat. You got any idea how big a tape recorder was back in them days? They didn't have no microcassettes, I'll tell you that much.

"But your mama, she was a pearl beyond price. She loved me and she stood by me and she did what she had to do to save me. She was the empress of my heart and there ain't been another woman like her then nor since."

Patrick drank from his beer again. "So what are you getting at, Dad?"

"I'm sayin' a man's gotta do what a man's gotta do."

"Well, that helps a lot. Thanks, Dad."

"And I'm remindin' you that you ain't got forever with this thing. If you wanna be ready when—"

"I know, Dad. I know."

"So what are you gonna do?"

Right then, Eden stuck her head through the curtain that led to the main room. "All right you two, feet off my table. Now."

Oggie groused, "Hell and damnation, even the tables are *hers* now." But he obediently swung his feet to the floor. Patrick followed suit.

"You guys want another beer?"

"It's all right, Eden. I'll get them," Patrick said.

"Oh, sit down. I'm *pregnant,* not disabled." She disappeared back into the main room.

Oggie looked at his middle son. "So, you gonna answer me or not? What the hell you gonna do?"

"I'm gonna be at the church picnic tomorrow, that's what. And I'm gonna wait. And watch."

"And be ready. Readiness is all."

Patrick pointed his beer at his father in a salute. "Gotcha, Dad. Readiness is all."

The next day Regina arrived at Sweetbriar Park before him, along with box after box of fresh-baked cookies. One of the duties she'd assumed was to see that everything was properly set up and to get the commercial barbecues going.

Her heart did a funny little flip-flop when Patrick drove up in a delivery truck just a little before eleven. He'd volunteered, it turned out, to bring over the donations of burgers, hot dogs and buns from the Mercantile Grill.

"Eden also asked me to stay and supervise the barbecues," he told her. "That okay with you?"

"That's just fine. Great, as a matter of fact." She hated the falsely bright sound of her own voice. "Um, let me know if there's anything you need."

"Right," he said. But his tone said he wouldn't ask her for the time of day.

Her spirits drooped, to have him speak to her so coldly, though she knew her reaction was completely out of line. She had snubbed him twice in the past week, going inside when he waved at her and pretending not to hear when he called to her.

However little she really knew him, she did know he was not stupid or lacking in perception. He understood exactly the message she'd sent him: keep away. She had no right to be droopy because he was giving her just what she'd asked for.

And she would *not* be droopy, she scolded herself. It was a beautiful day, and the park was green and lush, full of shady spots and warm pools of sunlight.

Marcus was coming at eleven-thirty, and she had promised to spend the day with him. They'd enjoy their meal and go on the treasure hunt together. Then they'd wander the bazaar tables, buying cute things they didn't need, and feeling good about spending their money because the money this year was to be used to put a new roof on the church. They'd hold hands. She would tease him into buying some of those dozens of cookies she had finished baking yesterday. When dark came, they would dance together by the light of the full moon.

Marcus arrived right on time, in a delivery truck with North Magdalene Grocery printed on the side. He had brought the dry goods and condiments from his store, as promised. Regina—and Nellie, who'd been there since ten—helped him to unload everything and set it out.

By that time, it was past noon. The smell of grilling hamburgers made Regina's stomach growl.

"You two go on and have fun," Nellie suggested. "I can handle whatever comes up from here on."

"You're sure?" Regina asked, to be polite.

"Certainly. I have oodles of help, and you've already done more than your share."

At that moment, Regina was so glad to be set free of responsibility for a while that she almost forgave Nellie for spreading tales about herself and Patrick Jones.

"Great. Thanks, Nellie." She grabbed Marcus's hand and towed him to her car, from which she produced a big blanket.

"Now, hurry," she told him with a conspiratorial wink. Then she raced to an area off to the side of all the activity that she'd had her eye on all morning, a nice grassy spot beneath a leafy chestnut tree. She spread the blanket there, pleased to be claiming the cool, somewhat secluded location before someone else did.

Marcus complained that they'd be more comfortable at a table, but she good-naturedly pooh-poohed him and led him to the ticket booth, where they purchased strips of tickets, which they could use to trade for food and anything else that caught their fancy.

After that, she dragged him over to where the food was set out. They each handed over the required number of tickets, and then Regina, laughing, tucked the remainder of her own tickets under the belt of the button-front sundress she'd bought specifically to please Marcus. It was the kind of dress Marcus liked: a simple, modest dress with a high collar and a subdued floral print.

Linda Lou Beardsly, who was supervising the food tables, gave them paper plates, which they proceeded to load up with all manner of potluck goodies.

"And I've got to have one of those hamburgers," Regina said, her plate already full.

"You don't have room," Marcus said, rather disapprovingly.

"I'll make room." She was laughing over her shoulder at him. "Come on, Marcus. Live dangerously. Get a burger, too."

"I'll pass," he said, backing up suddenly, looking beyond her shoulder, his expression wary.

She wondered what could be going through his mind, as she turned—and nearly bumped into Patrick Jones. He held a bun in one hand and a just-grilled hamburger patty on a spatula in the other.

"Here you go," he said.

"I . . ."

He set the bun on her plate gently, opening it with his tan fingers and edging it between a tossed salad with vinaigrette dressing on one side and something Linda Lou had called Potato Surprise on the other. Then he eased the patty onto the bottom half of the bun.

Regina watched Patrick's hands doing this simple series of actions, setting the bun on the plate, opening it, laying the meat on top. And she had that same feeling she'd had at her front door that morning a month ago, right after he moved in next door, when he came over to borrow the sugar for his father's coffee and she'd looked at his feet and thought how beautiful they were.

It was a feeling of sadness, of something splendid glimpsed too briefly, and then gone.

She looked up, into his waiting eyes. "Thank you."

"You're welcome."

And then he turned away.

She knew she stood staring at his proud back much longer than she should have. But it took time to return from that forbidden place into which she had somehow slipped while he was edging a hamburger bun onto her paper plate.

Over behind where the portable bandstand had been erected, someone set off a handful of firecrackers. The sound jarred Regina enough that she collected herself and looked around for Marcus. He was standing right where she'd left him, halfway between the food tables and the barbecue grills. His expression was not encouraging.

She pasted an unconcerned smile on her face and hurried to his side. "Let's get something to drink, shall we, before we head for the blanket?"

"Fine."

They went to the big metal tubs, which were filled with ice and soft drinks, and chose two cans of cola. Then they went to sit down.

Regina tucked her legs beneath the hem of her dress and concentrated very hard on her food. Marcus, beside her, was silent. She knew he was upset and she was hoping that, if she just ignored him for a little while, he would forget what had happened and they could go on with their lovely afternoon.

But deep in her heart, Regina knew such a wish was futile. It had only been a few moments in time, and all Patrick Jones had done was serve her a hamburger. And yet, when he turned away from her, she had, for endless seconds, been unable to turn away from him. Marcus, who she so wanted to love, had witnessed it all.

It was such a tiny thing. And yet its immensity terrified her.

"He's staring at you," Marcus said quietly.

Regina put up no pretense. She didn't ask "Who?" In fact, she didn't even want to look to see if what Marcus said was true. Yet she couldn't help herself. She raised her glance to the two pushed-together tables about twenty yards away where all the rowdy, passionate Joneses were sitting.

Patrick *was* looking at her.

And there was something in his look. A challenge—a taunt. It was completely crazy. It made no logical sense. But Regina Black knew at that moment that the life she had planned for herself was slipping from her grasp.

Since the morning Patrick Jones had moved in next door to her, her life, like a river at flood time, had been cutting a new channel for itself. Slowly at first, but with gathering momentum, she was being swept away. She was losing control, caught up in emotions and feelings the like of which she had never known.

Dangerous emotions, hazardous feelings . . .

"You encourage him," Marcus said, his voice low and very controlled. He didn't want anyone else to hear.

Regina made herself stop looking at Patrick, though it seemed to take every ounce of will she possessed. She stared down at her plate.

"I do not," she said between clenched teeth, and felt like the world's worst liar.

"You encourage him," Marcus repeated, soft but firm. "And what's more, you're in denial about it."

"I don't encourage him." She looked up once more, to glare at Marcus. "That isn't fair. I do *not* encourage Patrick Jones."

"My, my, you certainly are *vehement* about this."

"Vehement? Well, of course I'm vehement. I'm *not* looking at Patrick Jones, nor am I encouraging him. It's *you* I'm looking at, Marcus. And if you'd just—"

Marcus cleared his throat. She saw that he hated this, that it pained him terribly, both the way Patrick kept looking at her *and* her stuttered and awkward declaration of her feelings.

"Now, now, Regina," he muttered. "Let's not get carried away."

"Carried away?" Her voice rose, though she knew Marcus hated loud, rash displays. "Marcus, I'm trying to tell you I—"

"Hush." He patted her arm as if she were a skittish animal. "People are starting to stare at us." His eyes darted back and forth in their sockets. She could see he thoroughly regretted remarking on the situation with Patrick Jones, because now he was very close to becoming half of a public spectacle. He went on, "It was quite unwise of me to bring up this subject here, in a public place. I apologize."

Regina, humiliated, confused and now thoroughly miserable, subsided. She tried to eat her hamburger, but it stuck like sawdust in her throat.

She turned away in an effort to get her emotions back under control. As she did so, she locked glances with old Oggie Jones, who just happened to be tottering by at that moment on the cane he had walked with ever since he got careless with his hunting rifle and shot himself in the foot.

The old man smiled at her, a slow, crafty smile, just like the one he had granted her that first morning, when Patrick had moved in next door to her. The same morning when her life had begun its slow slide out of her control.

Her gaze still held by the old man's, Regina forced herself to swallow the dry wad of hamburger that didn't want to go down her throat.

In Oggie's beady black eyes, it seemed, she saw everything—how she had heard the voices and gone to her window. And from the moment she saw Patrick there, sweating and straining over that refrigerator, so ruggedly beautiful that it broke her heart, her life had taken a new, uncharted course. A course she had denied for a month now—just as Marcus had accused. But a course she was destined to follow, fight it though she might.

Unless . . .

Yes, she thought frantically. Unless she could force something different to happen. Right now. Today. Before it was too late.

She closed her eyes, to shut out the frightening old man. And when she opened them again, he had passed from her sight. Then, setting her half-eaten lunch aside, she turned to Marcus once more.

Marcus, with his gentle eyes and soft-spoken ways. Marcus, a man of whom even her mother might have approved. Marcus, her last link with her world as she knew it. Her last chance for a safe, uneventful, contented life.

"Marcus, I . . ."

His gaze shifted away, and then back. She knew with grim certainty that he had no desire to hear what she might say. Yet she had to try.

They were some distance from the other picnickers, and she was sure no one would hear what she said as long as she didn't let her voice get out of control.

She took great care to keep her tone low and unchallenging as she began, "Marcus, I . . . I want certain things in life. Can you understand that?"

"Now, Regina. Perhaps we—"

"Let me say this. Please."

"But, Regina, this is very public, and I—"

"Please. I'll keep my voice down. I promise." She waited. He didn't agree to hear her out, but he didn't call a halt, either. He merely looked pained.

She forged on. "Marcus, I want love, and marriage. Maybe children. And I . . . I want them with you. I keep hoping you'll say you care for me, Marcus. Do you, Marcus? Do you care for me?"

Marcus looked miserable. "Well, now, Regina. Of course I care for you."

Suddenly, watching him, she perceived the truth. What Regina Black wanted and what Marcus Shelby wanted were two very different things.

She knew his age, but she asked him anyway, "How old are you, Marcus?"

He blinked, puzzled. "You know. You gave me a birthday party only six months ago. I'm forty-three."

"And you've never been married."

"No, of course not. You know that."

"And you never intend to marry, do you?"

"Well, now, Regina—"

"Just say it, Marcus. Just get the words out of your mouth."

"Regina."

There was a coldness inside her at that moment, a frozen center of absolute ruthlessness. She scrambled to her feet, brushed off her skirt and demanded, so quietly, she herself could barely hear the words, "Say it."

Marcus gulped. And then he seemed to come to some sort of bleak decision within himself. He spoke very low, and very deliberately. "Okay, Regina. It's probably for the best if we're totally frank with each other anyway. I don't want to get married. I like being a bachelor. I like just what we have together. An important and meaningful relationship, where we both have our independence and our privacy."

She stared down at him, and she felt the coldness ease a bit, felt herself relax. A strange quietude was stealing over her.

"I see." Now she was the soul of reason. "Well, then, it looks like we're headed in different directions, Marcus. Because *I* want to get married. We want different things, and that's all there is to it."

"But, Regina—"

She put up a hand. "I've enjoyed your company, Marcus."

"Regina—"

"But I don't want to see you anymore. Will you please step off my blanket?"

"Listen, please . . ."

"Just step off of it, Marcus. Now."

Marcus watched her for a moment, and then shrugged. He rose, the movement awkward as he tried not to spill what was left on his plate. Once he was upright, he stepped aside. Swiftly and efficiently, Regina folded the blanket and stuck it beneath her arm. Then she bent to scoop up her own plate.

"Now what?" he asked.

She stood very straight. "I'm going for a walk right now into the woods alone. Don't follow me."

"Regina, don't be childish."

"Goodbye, Marcus."

She turned from him, her head high, and started walking away from the picnic area, into the trees. Behind her, she heard more firecrackers going off, then Pastor Johnson's sonorous voice over the loudspeakers, announcing the beginning of the big treasure hunt. She tossed the rest of her lunch in a trash can as she marched past it. Then she strode briskly, clutching her blanket, away from the picnic and the loudspeakers, away from Marcus's rejection of her, and from the knowing heat in the eyes of Patrick Jones.

At first she had some worry that Marcus might dare to follow, and that she would have to turn and insist that he leave her alone. But that didn't happen. As the sounds of the picnic faded, muffled by the distance and the thick branches of the trees, Regina knew she'd seen the last of Marcus Shelby, at least for now.

She walked on, through the trees, her canvas espadrilles crunching on pine needles, her head held high. She didn't know exactly where she was going, but she had a sort of numb, desperate feeling that as long as she kept putting one foot in front of the other, she wouldn't have to think about all the hopes she'd pinned on Marcus Shelby, and how those hopes had never had a chance of coming true.

Eventually, she found herself at the trail at the foot of Sweetbriar Summit, a hill that could be seen quite clearly from town. She hesitated there, at the base of the hill, thinking that her espadrilles weren't exactly suitable for climbing, and that the blanket would be an awkward burden to carry with her.

And then she decided she didn't care about her own unpreparedness. She felt compelled to continue. As if her fate were now mercilessly drawing her forward.

She put her foot on the trail, and she moved on.

For a while, it wasn't bad. The trail was clear and it crisscrossed back and forth across the slope of the hill, so the climb was not too steep.

But then the trail shot upward. Regina had to scramble, sometimes slipping, grabbing on to branches and roots, to keep from sliding back. She grunted and groaned, forging upward, feeling the sweat gather beneath her breasts and under her arms, staining her new dress. Her hair, which she'd pulled back into its usual neat bun that morning, came loose and straggled over her face. And often, in the shadowed places, there were swarms of gnats that got in her eyes and tried to fly into her mouth. More than once she fell forward, breaking her fall with the blanket that kept interfering with her balance, which was tenuous at best.

She knew she was being foolish to go on, especially when the trail petered out to nothing and she found herself scrabbling upward, on all fours most of the time, grabbing any rock or exposed root she could find to keep from tumbling off down the hill. She knew she should at least set the blanket down. Chances were she would be able to find it again on her return. And even if she didn't, it would be no great loss.

But something kept her going, sweating and straining, clutching the blanket, swatting at the gnats and muttering little exclamations of frustration and irritation under her breath.

And then, when she was almost ready to call it quits and turn around, out of nowhere, she was topping the crest. One minute, there was a grouping of serpentine boulders in front of her. The next, she scrambled over them and found herself in a tiny meadow, where buttercups and wild columbines bloomed. To her left, there was a little stream that bubbled up from an underground spring and tumbled off down the hillside not far away.

Regina froze, turned and looked around her, out over the river to North Magdalene, now shining in the afternoon sun like some picture postcard of the perfect mountain town. She could see the new spire on the recently refurbished bell tower of her church. She spotted the school where she worked part-time during the school year, and old Mrs. Leslie's house, where she went to help out so often during her afternoons. And there was Pine Street, her street, with Nellie's house and her house . . . and Patrick's house, too.

She could see it all from up here. But no one could see her.

Suddenly she felt giddy. She wondered if what had happened back at the picnic, and her wild scramble up the side of the hill, had unbalanced her mind a little.

And then she realized that she didn't care.

Regina smiled, a slow, secret smile. She knew a feeling she had never known: total freedom. An utterly delicious sensation.

She tossed her blanket to the grass. And she stretched her arms up and out, there beneath the wide sky. She tipped her head back and turned in circles until a sweet dizziness forced her to stop. And when she did stop, swaying with her head thrown back, waiting for her balance to return, she saw a hawk. It glided and circled, riding the air currents in search of unwary prey. She watched it for a time, until it soared too near the sun and she had to look away.

She went to the stream and drank of it, and freely splashed the clear, cool water on her heated face and neck. Then she went back to the blanket—a stroke of brilliance, not to leave the blanket behind—and she spread it on the grass half-in and half-out of the shade of an oak. She slipped off her dusty espadrilles and stretched out on her back on the sunny side of the blanket.

Her body felt good, well used, slightly heavy. Her breath sighed sweetly in and out.

Until the moment that she heard the soft rustle of footsteps in the grass, she did not consciously know that she was waiting.

Her eyes were closed against the sun, but then she felt a shadow block out the brightness.

She sat up, and saw that it was Patrick Jones, as some secret, primal part of her had known it would be. The sun was so bright that she had to shade her eyes to look at him. For a long moment, they stared at each other.

Then he asked in an offhand voice that belied the intensity in his eyes, "Seen a miner's pick around here?"

Regina frowned. The question, which seemed to have nothing to do with the reason her fate had brought him here, puzzled her.

He held up a map. "The treasure hunt. Remember? This is the spot where I'm supposed to find a miner's pick."

"Oh. Yes. Yes, of course." She tucked her bare feet under her and moved over a little, until she was in the shade of the oak.

He dropped to a crouch before her, still in the sun. She tried not to draw back any farther, but the reality of his presence overwhelmed her. She was so poignantly aware of him, of the lithe beauty of his fine body and the warmth coming off his tanned skin. In a bold move, she took the map from his hands.

She studied the mimeographed sheet, then lifted her head to meet his gaze. "This map stops halfway up the trail."

"It does?" His lips curled in a hint of a smile.

"You followed me."

He was silent for a moment. Now his eyes seemed to measure her. "Yeah, I followed you." He took the map away from her, crumpled it and tossed it aside.

She didn't let her gaze waver. "Why?"

"I saw you leave."

"That doesn't answer my question."

"Yeah, it does. I followed you because I saw you leave Marcus Shelby. And you looked like you weren't planning to come back." His eyes narrowed. "*Were* you planning to come back?"

Regina didn't answer. Her emotions kept changing, teetering on a razor's edge. Right then, she was angry again. Angry at Patrick Jones. Her life was slipping out of her control. And it was all this man's fault. "Are you through with Marcus Shelby?" Patrick asked, more directly this time.

Regina still wouldn't answer. She looked away, out across the mountains. So much had happened to her today. She'd admitted to herself that her life was changing. And she'd seen the truth about her loneliness and her unfulfilled dreams.

And she knew now that she had chosen Marcus precisely because he had not wanted any deep involvement. Marcus had been safe—safe to spin her shy, old-maid fantasies around. Until the day she looked out her window and saw Patrick Jones, she'd been content with her dreams that would never come true.

But then, the day had come. She had looked at Patrick, and his image had been seared into her mind and heart. And she had started changing. And what she wanted now was something that would have shocked her to her virgin core only a few weeks before.

Patrick took her chin in his hand, and made her look in his eyes once more. "Say it. Tell me."

She did not shrink from his touch. It was warm and rough and made her heart beat faster. It was what she wanted, and she was through hiding from what she wanted, from the truth. Today, the truth had burned the shyness right out of her. She looked in Patrick's eyes. "Yes. Marcus and I are through."

"Good." His thumb lazily stroked the soft skin of her jawline, causing lovely ripples of sensation that made her breath catch. "What you want he'll never give you anyway."

She felt a stab of anger at Patrick again, at his knowing the truth about Marcus so easily, when it had taken her until today to admit it to herself. "Oh, really?" Her tone was brittle.

He looked at her mouth. He was smiling. "Really."

"And just what *do* I want?"

His hand moved, his fingers threading through her tangled hair. "A husband," he said. "You want a husband and a family. You want marriage."

Suddenly her anger and bravado fled. She was frightened. He knew too much. Saw too much. She tried again to turn her head.

But he wouldn't let her go. "This was coming." His voice soothed. "Don't disappoint me. Don't lie to me and say you didn't know."

"But I didn't." Her gaze shifted away from his.

He let go of her chin. "Damn." He started to stand.

"Wait."

His eyes were on her, pinning her. "The truth. Or I'm gone."

She looked at him proudly. "I *am* telling the truth. I didn't know. Until today."

"What the hell does that mean?"

"It means I know now. It's all very clear now—in retrospect. But I . . . I wasn't able to admit it, until today."

Patrick looked at her, weighing what she'd said. It seemed to satisfy him. He dropped to his haunches again. "Okay, you're through pretending, then? Walking away when I wave to you, hurrying off when I call your name?"

She licked her lips. "Yes. I'm through doing those things."

"Good."

He reached for her again. His hand curled around the back of her neck, warm and firm and sure. She felt another quick stab of panic. "Patrick?" It was a plea.

"Shh." With stunning gentleness, he began removing what pins were left in her hair. He pulled them free and set them on the edge of the blanket in a neat, even row. And then he combed her hair down on her shoulders with his fingers. "There," he said, when he was done.

"I . . ." She had suddenly forgotten how to talk.

But it didn't seem to matter. He moved from a crouch to his knees, so close that his thighs were touching her curled-under legs. His thighs felt hard as heated steel against her. Regina shivered from that heat, and she knew the fiercest, most wonderful tumble of emotions.

Fear. Joy. Desire. Excitement.

He traced the side of her face with his hand. She shivered. He made a small, soothing sound in his throat. She swayed toward him, so that her upturned face was once more in the sun. And then he pushed his fingers through her unbound hair. He cupped the back of her head.

"You want a husband, marriage and a family," he repeated. "I know what you want."

She stared at him, and glimpsed the sun. It blinded her, so that afterimages, what her mother had always called sun dogs, began dancing in front of her eyes. She was . . . stunned. Stunned by her own feelings, by the gathered intensity in his body and by the waiting receptiveness in hers.

Patrick was still smiling, but the smile had a predator's edge now. She thought of the mountain lion, all those years ago. Of the way it had watched her, and then allowed her to go. She knew, with a fierce, frightened glee, that she would not be allowed to go this time. That she did not want to go this time.

"I know what you want, Regina," he said again. His face loomed closer. He blotted out the sun. "Marriage, children. A family. And this . . ."

His mouth covered hers.

Chapter Six

Regina moaned, a starved, startled sound that she didn't realize she'd made until she heard it echo in her head. Patrick gave the sound back to her. It was a mating sound, a sound of need, and demand.

For a split second, fear again took the upper hand. She jerked back from him, losing the consuming touch of his mouth.

They stared at each other. She shook her head.

He nodded.

Time went on forever, and yet stood still.

He didn't reach for her again. He waited.

"Oh, Lord," she murmured, "I cannot do this."

"You can. Close your eyes."

Where the courage came from, Regina had no clue. But she did as Patrick instructed. She let her eyelids close out the meadow and faraway picture-postcard town, the sun, the hawk—and Patrick Jones. Now there was only the dark velvet of her inner lids, and the sun dogs, still shifting and popping before her because she had glanced once or twice at the sun.

"Better?"

She nodded, lowering her head. The sun dogs danced outward, fading to the periphery of her darkened sight.

"Can I touch you?"

She bit her lip. And then nodded once more.

For a moment, nothing happened. She sat on the blanket, her senses tuned high, aware of the heat of the sun and the slight breeze, the smell of evergreen, and the presence of the man, so close to her.

And then he took her hand. He raised it, and pressed it to his lips. She moaned again at the contact. A single tear slid down her cheek.

He touched that tear with his free hand and smoothed it on her cheek until the summer wind cooled it and took it away.

"Don't be afraid, Regina." His voice was a caress in itself. It was the wind and the Summit, her freedom—all new. "It's your first time?"

From somewhere she found her voice. "Yes."

He said nothing, only opened her palm and put his mouth there. His lips moved and his teeth grazed lightly. Regina loosed a long sigh.

And then his hand slid up her bare arm, a long, learning caress. His other hand joined it as he took her face in both hands and pulled her toward him. He kissed her again, a discreet, exploratory caress, a very gentle breath of a kiss.

At first.

But within seconds, the kiss was deepening. "Part your lips for me," he whispered against her mouth.

Her lips went soft, opening of their own accord. And his tongue pressed its advantage, tasting her mouth and then sliding inside to know more of her than any man had ever known before.

She moaned and his hard arms closed around her. He urged her backward to lie upon the ground, guiding her so she lay beneath the cool shadow of the tree. She went, her body yearning, hungering for that which it had never experienced.

He lay full upon her for a moment, covering her, so she would know him, feel his length upon her, his hardness against her. And he kissed her, long and deep.

Then he eased himself over and lay at her side, so his hand was free to touch her. He went on kissing her, as he molded her waist and learned the curve of her hip with gentle, knowing strokes.

And then he pulled back. She groaned in protest because he'd stopped kissing her. She dared to open her eyes.

Above her, he was watching her, challenging her, as he had a million years ago down in the park at the church picnic. Challenging her to...

His hand was on the forgotten strip of tickets, which she'd tucked under the belt at her waist. He held her eyes as, very slowly, he pulled the tickets free. He raised them, until they dangled in a thin cardboard chain above her breasts.

"You may not get much use out of these," he warned. His voice was husky. "I might keep you here all day. Maybe I'll have to pay you back, for not getting your money's worth from them." He lowered the paper chain, until it touched her right breast, at the nipple. Beneath her bra and slip and her new dress, the nipple hardened. Sweet, melting sensations chased themselves around inside of her. "Would that be fair, Regina?"

"What?" The word was slow, melting like she was.

"For me to buy these tickets off of you?"

"No."

"Why not? Did Marcus Shelby buy them for you?" His expression, which had been so intense and knowing, closed a little. Even fogged as her mind was with desire, she noticed that slight change in him, though she didn't understand it.

But then, she thought, Patrick Jones wasn't the kind of man a woman easily understood.

"Answer me, Regina." There was a thread of steel now, underlying the velvet of his voice.

She drew in a breath, and then spoke in a tone that tried its best to be level, in spite of all the distracting sensations Patrick was creating with his nearness and his touch. "No. Marcus didn't buy them. *I* bought them. And even if I don't use them, I don't want my money back. It'll go to the church. I'm glad to see it put to use there." She felt a little guilty, speaking of the church while she lay beneath an oak tree with Patrick Jones. But she pushed the guilt aside. What would happen here would happen. Feeling guilty wouldn't change it.

The closed look left his face. He smiled his slow smile. "You're a good girl, aren't you?"

"I am not a girl."

He chuckled and lowered the tickets, until the whole chain of them lay in loops over her breasts.

She spoke more firmly. "I mean it. I'm not a girl."

"Yes, ma'am." Patrick gathered up the chain of tickets, his fingers brushing her breasts unconcernedly as he did it, causing little flashes of desire to explode like firecrackers inside her, making both of her nipples pucker and ache within the confines of her bra. He wadded the tickets and tossed them away, as he had the treasure map.

And then, very casually, he put his hand on her breast. He cupped it. She felt her nipple, hard and hungry, in the center of his palm. Her body, yearning for more, arched toward his hand through no will of her own.

"Yeah," he murmured. "Oh, yeah..." He rubbed her breast and found the aching nipple with his thumb. He flicked it gently, back and forth. She moaned, closing her eyes again, and tossed her head on the blanket.

As he explored her body, he whispered, "I knew you'd be like this. I knew there was fire under there. Secret fire. The very best kind. A fire for me, just me. It's what I've been needing for all my damn useless life, Gina. My own secret fire." His voice was husky, hungry-sounding. "You know what I mean?"

But he gave her no chance to answer. Instead, he cupped the sides of her breast, positioning it so it swelled full and high. Then he lowered his head and covered that breast, still clothed though it was, with his mouth. He let loose a long, slow breath of warm air.

Regina arched again as his sweet, hot breath flowed through her dress and her underwear, to drive her a little crazy, to make her moan.

"Yeah," he muttered once more, the sound roughly tender against her breast.

Then he lifted his head again, and his hand went to the row of buttons that traveled down the front of her dress. Sighing, her whole body seeming to have somehow turned liquid, Regina felt compelled to open her eyes.

Patrick was looking at her face, his own face flushed, his lips slightly swollen, his eyes languorous blue slits. He held her gaze, with that special lazy but insistent way he had, not letting her look away, as he began to undo the buttons.

One by one, the buttons slipped from their holes, until they were undone down to her waist. Very slowly, he parted the dress, revealing her plain white slip. She whimpered.

"Easy. We're going easy." He granted her one sweet kiss, a kiss both of promise and of reassurance.

And then his hand became insistent once more, guiding the bodice of the dress from her shoulders, so that it gathered at her waist, smoothing down her slip straps, and taking the slip down with her dress. Then he guided her bra straps over her shoulders, waiting until she pulled her arms free of them.

"Turn on your side. Let me unhook this thing."

She did as he asked, smoothing her hair out of his way. He undid the back clasp. She closed her eyes again, holding the bra against her breasts, her whole body burning to feel more of the sweet sensations his touch brought. Yet she couldn't quite bring herself to turn back to him and let him see her naked to the waist here beneath an oak tree in the middle of the afternoon.

He must have sensed her anxiety, because he didn't urge her to turn. Instead, he wrapped his hard arms around her and pulled her back against him, spoon fashion.

For endless moments, they lay still. She felt his breath against the curve of her neck. He allowed her to become used to him, holding her with her bottom tucked against his sex, which she could feel was very much aroused. His strong thighs cradled her, his big arms seemed, in the way they held her, to speak to her of safety, of a haven from all fears.

And then he began to stroke her again, first caressing her bare waist, then sliding his hand up, beneath the bra which she was still clutching against herself.

"Let it go, Gina. Let me touch you. Please."

Her hands relaxed. Carefully, he took the bra away. Then he kissed her shoulder, as his hand cupped her breast, naked for him at last. She dared to look down, to see the strong, brown hand around her small, pale breast. She hitched in a shocked gulp of air, and squeezed her eyes closed.

He went on touching her breast, cupping it, arousing the nipple as he put his lips on her neck. He sucked lightly, moaning a little, nipping and nibbling her skin.

It seemed she was awash in him. His scent, like musk and cedar shavings and something else—dust and sunshine?— swam all around her. His body surrounded her. His hands and mouth claimed her. She sighed and let her head relax in the crook of his arm as her hips began moving in a rhythm she hadn't even realized she knew, rocking in building need against him. He moaned louder, and his body pressed back and forth in rhythm with hers.

His hand left her breast, strayed downward, over her bare upper belly, to where the tops of her dress and slip were bunched around her waist. His hand slid lower still. She stiffened.

He licked her neck, then blew on it. "Let me touch you," he said again. "I'll give you a climax, first. It will make it easier. Later."

She moaned and rubbed her cheek against his arm. She yearned. And she needed. And yet, to hear him say that, say what he'd do, shocked her to her very toes.

When she didn't answer, he took charge. His hand found its way beneath her skirt and slid between her soft thighs. Then it trailed up over her stomach, only to dip lower once more, to delve beneath the elastic waist of her cotton panties. Her belly jumped, and she stiffened as she felt his touch, gentle yet relentless, on her most private place.

"I—"

"Shh. Feel, Gina. That's all. Just feel."

"But..."

His fingers parted her. She groaned.

"Yeah. Feel. That's right..."

His fingers began to move. She could not believe the things his fingers did. She forgot her own embarrassment, she forgot everything. Her hips found that heretofore unknown rhythm once more. His hand stroked her, following the cues her body gave it.

There was a flickering feeling of wonder. It receded and then approached again, receded and approached. She was moaning, tossing her head. She could hear herself, whimpering, pleading.

And he was stroking her, whispering, "Yeah," his body pantomiming the frantic actions of hers, moving in tandem with her, urging her on.

The wonder approached again, this time like a huge wave. It rose up and rolled over her, consuming her. She threw back her head against his hard chest and cried aloud.

The wave crested and she rode it, high, glorious, frantic. She felt her secret place contracting, right where he was stroking her. She knew that he felt it; she heard his triumphant groan.

And then, as the aftertremors still shook her, he was pulling her onto her back. She went where his hands guided her. At that moment she was totally, completely his. He could have done just about anything. She knew he saw her breasts, bare and pale in the daylight. And it was fine. They were *his* breasts right then. Her entire body, her being, was his.

Quickly, his gaze focused and yet glazed, he unhooked her belt and unbuttoned her dress the rest of the way down. He pulled it out from under her, tossed it aside and took her slip and panties, too, sliding them over her hips, off and away. Within seconds, she was naked before him as he knelt between her thighs.

He murmured, "Mine," and she did not gainsay him, though since her mother had died, she had taken great pride in belonging only to herself.

But the words he said didn't matter. This was what was meant to happen and she had surrendered to it, to her relentless fate. Her fate that had a name: Patrick Jones. She looked up at him, feeling no shame lying naked there with only the shade of the old oak to cover her, as he calmly stripped off his shirt and jeans, his lace-up boots and socks.

When he was naked, too, he loomed above her, the roof of oak leaves beyond his head. His beauty stunned her, as it had that first day. His chest was deep, his belly corded, his hips hard and narrow. He was fully, magnificently aroused.

He put his hand on her again, intimately, and the touch stunned her at the same time as she yielded to it. He stroked her, making her as ready as he could, given the fact that this was her first time.

And then he lowered himself, positioning himself between her pale thighs. She felt him straining at her and she knew she wanted to feel him fully inside her, at the same time as she knew it would cause her pain.

"I could make you pregnant," he said.

She blinked, surprised. What a fool she was. Of course. Doing what they were about to do could make a baby.

She got out, "I didn't . . ."

"It's okay with me," he said, when her voice trailed off. "I like babies."

She moaned a little. She was so utterly aroused, she could hardly think. Yet she knew that this subject, the subject of babies, was something they should deal with before what was about to happen took place.

"I, um . . ." She licked her lips.

And when her tongue came out, his eyes changed, heated even more. He put his hand over her mouth and lifted his brows. She licked his hand, as he seemed to be signaling for her to do.

"Ah...yeah..." Balanced on one arm, he tossed his head back as her tongue caressed his palm. His hardness pushed against her, parting her, so he was just a little bit inside, but stopped by the membrane that constituted her innocence. She could feel how wet she was, and how ready. She wanted him. She would give anything to have him fully inside her, to know what this most mysterious of acts was all about, and to know it with Patrick Jones.

But what would she do if, when they came down from Sweetbriar Summit, she carried his baby? The thought sent an unpleasant shiver through her. She'd always dreamed she might someday have children and the years were going by quickly. But she didn't know how she'd handle being pregnant and unmarried in a town like North Magdalene, while at the same time she could never imagine leaving there. It was and always would be her home. She turned her head, away from the palm that she'd been so lasciviously teasing with her tongue.

But he didn't let her go. His hand captured her chin again. He made her look at him. "I said before, Regina. I know what you want."

She opened her mouth to speak, though she didn't really know what she meant to say.

But he wasn't finished. He went on before she could begin. "I'll give you what you want. I'll give you this." He pressed a little deeper into her, stretching her tender inner flesh as far as it would go. One strong thrust would put him beyond the barrier. It would take her virginity, would take them both past the point of no return.

"I'll give you *all* of what you want. Babies. Starting now, if that's what happens from what we do here today. All you have to do is..."

She stared up at him, pleading with her eyes to know what he was asking of her.

He told her. "Marry me."

Chapter Seven

"Marry me." He said it again.

"I..."

"Say yes. Say it now, or—"

"But, I..."

"Say *yes,* Regina."

His eyes above her seemed like small pieces of the big, big sky. They went on forever, mesmerizing her. His body called to hers. And her body was answering. The strength of his purpose overwhelmed her.

How could she even for a moment have thought him less than frightening? How could she have been lulled by the touch of his hands to forget what he was: a wild, rough Jones. A man who would stop at nothing to claim what he wanted, no matter how implausible what he wanted might be—like marrying Anthea Black's sickly old maid daughter.

For a brief flash of time, she wanted to strike out at him, to roll from beneath him and run down the hill naked—anything, to escape him. To get away from the hard blue command of his eyes.

"Don't..." There was hurt in his voice, suddenly. He was pleading with her not to run.

And all her gathered rigidness fled.

The reality of her fate returned. Though she knew it would hurt her, she wanted him. He had called her his. And she was.

And if she married him, *he* would be *hers*.

Regina was not a fool. She knew Patrick didn't love her, that he must have some ulterior motive in this. But on the other hand, what he wanted and what she wanted were the same, really. She wanted a husband. And he was demanding that she marry him.

She looked up at the man poised above her. Her whole life spun around in her head. The town they both lived in. Who he was. Who she was. What an uproar there would be. That gorgeous hell-raiser Patrick Jones and plain, spinsterish Regina Black. Nellie Anderson and Linda Lou Beardsly would have a gossipmonger's jubilee.

"Marry me."

It was a crazy idea. An impossible idea.

He groaned. "Regina ... you'll kill me. Say you'll marry me, before I—"

Her answer came on a soft exhalation. "Yes."

His eyes changed again. They burned hotter, with triumph. He whispered, "Say it again."

"Yes." She lifted her arms and twined them around his neck. "Yes, yes, yes..."

And he thrust into her.

She threw her head back and cried aloud.

He thrust again, burying his head against her neck, moaning, "So good, so good..."

She held on, riding it out, though her untried body was too shocked by his invasion to begin the climb to fulfillment again. And he was lost to all but his own desire. She could feel it in the way he pushed into her, as if he must bury himself fully within her, as if he must brand her in her deepest place.

He rode her hard and fast. She clung to him, hearing her own woman's cries of mingled hurt and need and encouragement, clutching his broad back, aware of everything and nothing, as at last he thrust even deeper than all the thrusts that went before. His head, which he had buried against her shoulder, reared back. He howled his release at the oak and the meadow, at the wide summer sky, his neck straining, his hard arms braced on the blanket on either side of her.

When he was done, he hung his head and his body went lax, though he did not sink down upon her. A drop of sweat trickled from his hair and landed on her breast. Gently he dipped his head and licked it away.

Something melted inside her at the touch of his tongue. Deep in her heart, a tender space was created that hadn't been there before. She didn't examine it, she just *felt* it. And silently welcomed it.

"Regina." His eyes were waiting for hers. She met them. "I was rough, I hurt you."

"Yes." She reached up and stroked his damp hair back from his forehead.

"I should have been gentler."

She smoothed the hair at his temple, guiding it behind an ear. "No. You shouldn't. It was...what it was. Exactly perfect." She was thinking of fate, thinking that there was pain in one's fate, as well as glory. And that was what it had been. Painfully glorious. "It was just exactly right," she said aloud.

He let out a laugh that was really more like a groan, and then he very carefully retreated from her. He rolled to his back beside her and threw an arm over his eyes.

Regina, who hadn't felt naked at all while Patrick's body covered hers, suddenly felt very bare indeed.

She sat up bolt upright, spied her dress and grabbed it against herself—and then noticed the streaks of blood, drying now on the blanket and on her pale skin.

"Come on, we'll take care of that," Patrick said.

She started a little at the sound of his voice. Glancing over, she saw he was watching her. And then, in a fluid, stunning movement, he gathered his legs beneath him and stood.

He looked down at her. She thought how beautiful he was—and how comfortable with his own nudity.

Regina, on the other hand, was not comfortable at all. She sat staring up at him, clutching her dress against her breasts, trying not to notice that there were streaks of blood on his thighs, too.

He reached down for her. Not knowing what else to do, she gave him her hand. He pulled her up, while she held her dress tightly against herself.

Patiently, he pried her dress from her clenched fists, shook it out and held it up for her, open, the way a man holds a coat for a woman to slide into. She put her arms in the armholes and felt marginally more at ease the minute the dress was around her. He buttoned her up.

As he did that, she remembered her bra and her panties. "My underwear..."

"You don't need it. At least not right now."

"But..."

He buttoned the last button, then took her hand. "Come on."

He led her to the stream, where he let go of her hand and stepped into the narrow channel himself. He rinsed his body clean, pretending to pay great attention to what he was doing, though she knew he was really giving her a chance to wash herself without feeling that he watched her.

She gathered her skirt above her knees, waded in and rinsed off the telltale signs of her lost virginity. Then she quickly clambered up the mossy bank and returned to the blanket.

Once there, she had no idea what to do next. It was as if a fog were lifting. And what she had just done with Patrick Jones was seeming less and less like fate with each moment that passed.

Yes. Less and less like fate. And more like a huge and terrible, thoroughly humiliating mistake.

She grabbed up her panties and shimmied into them. Then, her back turned to Patrick who was still at the stream, she unbuttoned her dress to her waist and put on her bra, fumbling with it a little, but at last hooking the clasp, yanking it into place, pulling it up over her shoulders and shoving her arms through the sleeve holes of the dress once more.

Casting a guilty glance at her wadded-up slip, she hastily buttoned up again. She felt half-naked without the slip, but there was no way she was going to take off her dress again to put it on.

She would just have to roll the slip up in the blanket and hope that nobody noticed. Now, where was her belt?

She turned to look for it. And saw it dangling from Patrick's hand.

Her eyes widened. Somehow he had returned from the stream without her hearing him, while her back was turned and she was trying her best to make herself decent. He'd also managed to slip into his jeans.

"This what you're looking for?" He held out the belt.

"Y-yes, it is." She took it cautiously, the way one might take a shoe from the mouth of a dog known to bite. "Thank you."

Swiftly she wrapped the belt around her waist and buckled it. "Now, where are my shoes?"

He bent down. "Right here." He straightened, holding the espadrilles. She reached for them.

He held them away. "Wait a minute."

She frowned. "Excuse me?"

"I said wait a minute."

She didn't like his tone, not one bit. "Those are *my* shoes."

"No one said they weren't."

"Then give them to me."

"In a minute. When you're calmer."

"What do you mean?"

"I'm afraid if I give them to you now, you'll shove your feet in them and then turn and run."

That was exactly what she had been planning to do. She bit her lip. Her chin was quivering. Like a complete fool, she hovered on the verge of tears. She bit her lip harder, to make the tears recede. "This is ridiculous. You have absolutely no right to keep my shoes from me."

"Settle down." He sounded like someone trying to calm an hysterical woman.

Which wasn't too surprising. She was right on the brink of *being* an hysterical woman.

She looked away, out over North Magdalene, and collected herself, reminding herself that what had been done was done. She couldn't go back. Nothing would be served by indulging in an embarrassing crying jag right here in front of Patrick Jones.

"Regina." His voice was so gentle, it made her want to cry all over again. "Regina, I know this is a lot for you to take in all at once."

She forced herself to look at him again. "I must... I need to be alone now."

He seemed to study her. "All right." Then he advised, "But we'll be leaving tonight."

She stared at him. "Tonight? What are you talking about? Leaving for where?"

"For Tahoe."

"To do what?" she asked, though of course she knew what the answer must be.

"To get married." His chestnut brows lifted. His half smile had an ironic edge. "You do remember that you said you'd marry me. Don't you?"

"Yes. Yes, of course. I remember."

"Good."

"I do remember. But..."

"But what?"

She focused on the impossibility of the arrangements, in order *not* to think of the preposterousness of what she'd promised to do. "This is the Fourth of July weekend. Surely all the hotels will be fully booked."

"My dad has a few old friends there. He'll see to it we get a room."

"Oh...well..." Regina felt a slight headache begin at her temples. She pressed her fingers there and rubbed.

"We're going, Regina," Patrick said. He looked up toward the sun. "It's around three now. We'll leave at six."

"But I..."

"What?"

"I just..."

"What?"

"Well, I don't understand why we have to be in such a terrible rush about this."

He tossed her shoes at her feet. "Let's stop dancing around the real issue here. You agreed to marry me. Are you breaking your word?"

Suddenly she couldn't look at him.

"Regina, are you backing out?"

She shot him a quick glance. His face was hard, his eyes cold jewels.

She looked down again, this time at the blanket, where the blood of her innocence had dried now to a few rusty streaks. It was difficult to tell for sure now whether the streaks actually were blood.

But she knew what they were. Would always know.

Today she had crossed a boundary. And she had crossed it with this blue-eyed hellion.

"Regina." His voice commanded an answer.

She furiously considered.

The change in her life had come. She could embrace it, or hide from it.

As Anthea Black's daughter, she'd done a lot of hiding in her life.

Perhaps it was time to try a new way.

"Regina." His tone said he would not be put off any longer.

She looked right at him. "All right."

"All right, what?"

"All right, I'm not backing out. I'll marry you as I said I would."

His hard expression relaxed. "Okay." He nodded. "Okay."

She thought of the big church wedding she'd always dreamed of having. "But I don't see why we have to race off to Tahoe this very night. I'd rather—"

He raised a hand. "Some things, we'll do your way. But this, we'll do the way *I* want it. We've agreed to get married, and we're going through with it. Now. We're not going to hang around this town and give everyone a chance to screw things up. I know you can get away. The only real job you have is during school term, so now you're pretty flexible. Right?"

"Yes. But, Patrick, I—"

"You said you needed some time alone. You're wasting that time." He dropped to the blanket and pulled on his socks and boots. "I'll go and see that the arrangements are made." He briskly laced up his boots. "Plan to be gone till midweek. I wish it could be longer, but right now I can't leave the garage for any extended period of time. In a few years, maybe, we'll take off together for a real honeymoon." He grabbed his shirt, tossing it over his shoulder as he stood. "You want me to take the blanket back for you?"

"No, I, um..."

He grinned. "You're afraid someone will recognize it and figure out what we've been doing."

"Um, well, I..."

"Hey. It's okay." He shrugged. "I'll come for you. Six o'clock. Be ready." And then he turned and started down the hill.

She watched him go, a thousand arguments and questions bouncing around in her head. But she didn't stop him. She *did* want some time to herself. And he had not given her a lot of it. The opportunity to ask him questions would come soon enough.

After all, they were going to be spending the rest of their lives together.

At the very thought that she would spend the rest of her life with Patrick Jones, Regina's knees went a little weak. She sank to the blanket, landing on something that made a rustling sound. Paper. She scooted aside and found the wadded treasure map and the chain of picnic tickets.

She held them up, looked at them for a moment and then she clutched them to her breast. She loosed a long sigh, closed her eyes and tipped her face to the sky.

Then she slid them in her pocket and put on her shoes, after which she did her best to pin up her tangled hair.

When Regina reached the park once more, neither Patrick nor Marcus was anywhere in sight. She was grateful for that. She didn't even want to look at Marcus and she was mindful of the few hours Patrick had allowed her before their new, improbable life together would begin.

She'd almost reached her car when it occurred to her that tomorrow was Sunday. If she eloped with Patrick tonight, she would not be in church to play the hymns. She knew she must ask someone to see that other arrangements were made.

Nellie, as the church secretary, was the logical choice. But Nellie was the last person she wanted to talk to right now.

"Regina, are you all right?"

Regina blinked and realized she'd almost barreled into Delilah Fletcher. "What? Oh, yes. I'm fine. Just fine."

Delilah let out a throaty laugh. The laugh surprised Regina. Delilah never used to laugh like that—not until she got together with Sam, anyway.

"Well, you look positively wild," Delilah said.

Nervously, Regina smoothed her hair, which she knew she hadn't pinned up very effectively. "I do?"

Now Delilah smiled. "Yes. But it suits you."

"I—" It suddenly occurred to Regina that Delilah might be just the one she was looking for. "Delilah . . ." She took the other woman's arm and pulled her behind a tree. "I must have a word with you."

Delilah freed her arm from Regina's grip. "About what?"

"I just . . . I can't explain right now. But I won't be at church tomorrow. And someone must be found to play the hymns. Do you think you could ask Wilma Higgins? Or even Tondalaya Clark? Either Nellie or the pastor can give you the list of songs."

"Has this got anything to do with my brother, Patrick—and my father, perhaps?"

"Er, why do you ask?"

"About fifteen minutes ago, Patrick, who'd disappeared just after lunch, showed up. He whispered in my father's ear and then the two of them took off together."

"Well, Delilah, I—"

Delilah threw up both hands. "Never mind. Now that I think about it, I don't want to know. Of course I'll see to it that someone else can play the hymns."

"Oh, thank you."

"It's all right."

"I . . . I must go now."

"I understand." Delilah's dark eyes were soft. Regina smiled at her and turned away. "Regina?"

She turned back. "Yes?"

"Good luck. You'll need it."

For a moment, the two women looked at each other.

Then Regina nodded. "I know." She whirled and went on her way again, barely hearing Pastor Johnson announcing that the treasure hunters had exactly fifteen minutes left to report to the grandstand and that the bake sale auction would begin in one hour.

At her car Regina reached in the open window to pop the trunk latch. Then she went around to the back to toss the blanket in.

Just before she got there, she came face-to-face with Nellie.

"There you are, Regina. I've been looking all over for you."

Regina held back a groan. "Oh, hello, Nellie."

Trying to communicate an air both offhand and yet much too busy to hang around and chat, Regina edged around Nellie's tall, thin form. With great care she set the blanket in the trunk. Her slip, after all, was rolled inside it.

"Regina, we need you at the food tables now. Linda Lou is simply perishing for a break."

After shutting the trunk, Regina tried to edge around Nellie again, but Nellie quite openly stepped to block her path. Regina sighed. "Nellie, something's come up. I have to go home."

Nellie's eagle eyes were narrowed. "Why, dear, you seem to have acquired a *bruise.*"

Regina coughed. "Excuse me?"

"There. On your neck. You have a bruise. And your hair..."

"I went for a walk." Regina held her hand rigidly at her side, to keep it from rising and touching the place on her neck where she knew Patrick had kissed her while he held her spoon fashion against his chest. She hadn't even realized he'd left a mark.

"A *walk?*" Nellie looked frankly disbelieving.

Regina dragged her traitorous mind back from thoughts of Patrick's kisses. It was a major effort. "Yes, a walk," she said. "Quite a long, strenuous walk, actually. I'm sure I look frightful. And I...bumped into a tree."

Nellie's thin lips flattened. She didn't buy that for a moment. But there was kindness in Nellie, and it showed in her voice when she asked, "Are you all right?"

"I'm fine."

"Has someone hurt you?"

"No. Of course not. But I must go. Now."

Nellie's clawlike hand closed over Regina's forearm. "What has happened, Regina? You can trust me. You can talk to me."

Regina, who longed only to jerk free, ordered her body to relax. "Nellie—" she forced a mild tone "—you are so kind. And I do know exactly how much I can trust you. But there's nothing to talk about. I've become overtired, from walking, that's all. And I've worked so hard all week, on the picnic. Honestly, those twenty dozen cookies about did me in."

"Well, I—"

Gently Regina pulled her arm free of Nellie's clutching grasp. "I just want to go home and lie down for a while." That part was the truth. "And then, if I feel a little better, I'll be back. I promise you." A total lie, but Regina refused to be ashamed.

Sometimes one had to take extreme measures when dealing with Nellie. And Nellie would have the whole story soon enough, Regina had no doubt. But Regina was staunchly determined that Nellie would not get it from her.

Suddenly, the idea of disappearing from town for a few days held great appeal. By the time she returned, she would bet her piano, everyone would know that she and Patrick had eloped. And maybe that was just as well. She wouldn't have to explain it all in detail to everyone she talked to.

"Something's happened between you and Marcus, hasn't it?" Nellie looked appropriately consoling.

Regina considered. Perhaps the best way to get rid of Nellie right now would be to give her some intriguing little rumor to spread around. "Yes, Nellie. Something *has* happened between Marcus and me."

"Oh, I knew it. I just knew it." Nellie's eyes sparkled with eagerness. "What is it?"

"It's very simple. Marcus and I have discovered we want different things from life. We won't be seeing each other anymore."

"No!"

"Yes, I'm afraid that's the way it is. And now, I—"

Nellie leaned in close. "What 'different things' do you want?"

"Nellie—"

"You must talk about it, dear. You must get it all off your chest."

Regina sagged against her car and allowed herself to look exactly as worn-out and overwrought as she felt. "Nellie, I simply cannot talk about it now."

Nellie tipped her head to the side. She gave a small sigh. She was accepting the fact that she wasn't going to get any more out of Regina. For now.

It was time to lay the groundwork for the next assault. Nellie became all solicitude. "Well, of course you can't talk about it now." She patted Regina's shoulder. "You go on home and rest. And don't even *think* about coming back here today. You've simply been through too much. I'll handle everything."

I'm sure you will, Regina thought. "Thanks, Nellie."

"Don't even mention it." Nellie took Regina's arm as if Regina were aged or in some other way infirm, and helped her the few steps to her car door. Once inside, Regina reached under the seat for her small purse and found her keys.

Nellie closed the car door for her. "You just relax, now. Don't think about any of it. I'll call and check on you as soon as I get home today."

"Thanks, Nellie." Regina did her best to sound as if she meant it. "But today I'm not answering the door no matter what. And I'm taking the phone off the hook."

Nellie's face fell, but she managed to control her disappointment at not being able to pry more information out of Regina in the very near future. She clucked. "Of course, dear. I'll drop by tomorrow."

"Oh, Nellie. You don't have to bother with me. I'll be fine, really. I—"

"Nonsense. What are friends for? You just go home. Draw the blinds and get some rest. You can tell me everything in the morning."

There was no way Regina was going to reply to that one. She started up her car, gave Nellie a last wave, backed out and drove away.

The first thing Regina did when she reached her house was to rush to her bathroom and look at herself in the mirror over the sink. What she saw was a pale-skinned woman with wild brown hair and a love bite on her neck.

The pale skin flushed rosy pink. When Nellie found out that she'd eloped with Patrick Jones, then Nellie would figure out where that suspicious *bruise* had come from.

Regina lifted her chin. So what? By the time the town gossips started putting things together, she would be Patrick's wife. People like Nellie might not exactly approve of love bites, but they couldn't really condemn them if they were put there by a woman's legal spouse.

Regina went on staring at herself. For so many years, she had thought of herself as Anthea Black's daughter. Recently, she had begun to discover who she—Regina—was.

And now, though she was determined never to let another person control her life again, she would be more than the independent adult self she had discovered. She would also be Patrick's wife.

Patrick's wife.

Regina was stunned all over again, just thinking about it. She sank very slowly to the commode and stared at the potted philodendron on the windowsill.

When she felt she could stand again, she rose and removed her rumpled clothes and took a long bath. The water burned a little, when it touched the sensitive, newly used place between her thighs. She was tender there. But it was a good kind of tenderness. And now that she would be a wife, she would grow accustomed to lovemaking. The discomfort would fade.

Realizing that she was staring dreamily at the tub fixtures, Regina submerged herself completely in the water, after which she sat up and reached for the shampoo. She mustn't get too carried away with sentimental notions. She and Patrick had much to say to each other.

They had agreed to marry, but their courtship had been, to put it generously, brief. She knew very little of what he expected of her as his wife. And not much more about what she herself would want from him as her husband. She did realize that the tranquil existence she had pictured with Marcus would be highly unlikely with a man like Patrick Jones.

They would talk about it, Regina decided as she dunked her head again to rinse it. One of the most important things in a marriage, she firmly believed, was good communication. She would get some answers right away, especially about those ulterior motives she knew he must have for marrying her.

Chapter Eight

Regina's doorbell rang at exactly six o'clock. She was packed and ready, wearing a pink sleeveless dress with a V-neck and matching belt and shoes. It was a sexier dress than the conservative ones she usually wore.

In fact, over the past few years, she'd bought herself almost a whole new wardrobe of dresses, along with the appropriate accessories. She'd worn one or two of her new outfits when she'd begun dating Marcus. Very tactfully, Marcus had told her that the dresses didn't suit her. So she'd stopped wearing them.

Until now.

Now, every dress in the garment bag that she was taking to Tahoe was one of the newer ones.

She went to the door and pulled it open. Patrick was standing there, so handsome in tan slacks and a sports shirt, it almost hurt to look at him.

He gave her the kind of once-over men gave other women all the time.

"Yeah," he said.

She blushed and felt wonderful. Then she remembered her manners. "Won't you . . . come in?"

Patrick stepped past the threshold and she shut the door behind him.

He looked at her, his gaze lazy and hot. "You're something. I was half-afraid you'd chicken out on me, that I'd have to take drastic measures to get you in the car with me. But look at you. Just look the hell at you."

Shamelessly she inquired, "What kind of 'drastic measures?'"

He stuck his hands in his pockets and faked an innocent air—as he backed her up against the door. "Kidnapping, maybe. Or begging on my hands and knees." He brought his face very close to hers. "Or maybe . . ."

"Maybe what?"

He kissed her—a long, slow, bone-dissolving kiss. But he kept his hands in his pockets the whole time.

And when she was right on the brink of begging him to take his hands from his pockets and use them as only he knew how, he pulled away.

"All ready to go?" he asked in a voice that was probably a little hoarser than he meant it to be.

She noticed that his hair was wet and his face freshly shaven. She liked the smell of his after-shave. And she found it all incredibly endearing, to think of him grooming himself so thoroughly to be ready for his wedding trip. To look nice for her.

"I like your hair down like that," he said.

It covered the love bite, but she didn't say so. She only smiled. "Thank you."

"Well?"

"Yes?"

"I asked if you were ready."

"I am. Yes. Ready."

"Where's your stuff?"

"Right behind you. You almost tripped on it when you came in."

He put his hand on the door, near her head, and leaned on it. "I did not almost trip. I never almost trip. I'm a Jones."

"Yes. I know." A little thrill shivered through her. In North Magdalene, most women dreamed that one of the Jones boys might turn his eyes to her. The daring women dreamed openly. The more conservative types, like Regina, only dreamed such things in their most secret hearts.

"Your eyes are gray," he said. "Dove gray. But when you're turned on, they darken. Did you know that?"

"No, I . . ."

He leaned closer—and then pulled back. "We'd better get the hell out of here. Now."

"Yes, I—"

He turned and scooped up her suitcase, vanity case and garment bag. "Open the damn door."

She did as he told her. He went out ahead of her, leaving her to lock up.

When they turned onto Main Street, they found it nearly deserted. Regina assumed that everyone was still at the picnic across the river.

It did turn out, though, that Angie Leslie, old Mrs. Leslie's beautiful, thrice-divorced granddaughter, just happened to be coming out of Marcus's grocery store at the exact moment that Patrick and Regina drove by. Angie was carrying a full brown bag, and she almost dropped it on the sidewalk when she saw Regina Black sitting in the passenger seat of Patrick Jones's Ford Bronco.

Regina, not knowing what else to do, raised her hand in a wave. Angie shifted the bag in her arms and waved back. Patrick drove on by. Angie's mouth was still hanging open when Regina lost sight of her in the Bronco's side-view mirror.

Once the town was well behind them, Regina decided it was time to find out from Patrick exactly why he'd decided to make her his wife. She suggested they ought to talk about their reasons for getting married.

Patrick agreed that would be a good idea. Why *had* she agreed to marry him?

She sighed, thinking she should have been more direct. "But, Patrick, you already know my reasons. You listed them for me, up on Sweetbriar Summit a few hours ago, before you, um . . ."

"*Kissed* you," he provided, and then shot her a teasing grin.

"Right." She grinned back, feeling deliciously naughty, a wholly new sensation for her. "So now I'd like to know *your* reasons for marrying *me.*"

"Sure." He glanced in his side-view mirror, and then back out the windshield. "But first I'd really like to hear *your* reasons from you."

She frowned. This wasn't going at all as she'd imagined. "Patrick, if you already know them, why do I have to say them?"

"Because I'd like to hear them in your own words."

"But I—"

"I honestly would, Regina."

"Well, I . . ."

"Come on."

She realized he did have a point. It was only fair that she should explain her motives if she wanted him to detail his.

So she gamely began, "I, um, really want to be married, Patrick. I want a family. Working together with a man to build a good life is important to me. But until my mother died, I didn't realize that."

"Why not?"

"Well, my mother was a very demanding person." She slid him a glance, expecting him to make some humorously critical comment about her mother. Her feelings about her mother were not all positive. Yet she had loved her mother, and loyalty made her defensive when people made disparaging remarks about Anthea.

He noticed her glance, smiled at her and turned his eyes back to the road. "You never had a life of your own, did you, until she died?"

His voice was kind. He was such a fascinating man, really. He could be quite crude. And then he could stun her with his sensitivity.

"That's true," she said. "Until my mother died, my life was completely wrapped up with hers. She was so strong-willed. And I was all she had. She brought me up to be everything to her. And I loved her. But after I grew up, she just would not let me go. And I suppose I clung to her, too. When she died, I was *forced* to make my own life." She fell into a pensive silence, and then remembered her original subject. She sat up straighter. "Now, where was I?"

"After your mother died, you realized you wanted to get married."

"Yes. That's right. But I also wanted to live in North Magdalene, where my prospects were somewhat limited."

"Because?"

"You know very well why."

"So? Tell me anyway. Please?" The quick look he gave her melted her heart.

"Oh, all right. There were perhaps eight or nine unmarried men who were anywhere near my age. They were not breaking down my door to ask me out. But then Marcus bought the grocery store. He seemed such a nice, quiet, reserved man. A person just like me. We started dating. I assumed that eventually he would become my husband." She looked down and smoothed her dress over her knees. The memory of her humiliation with Marcus was still fresh.

"He never would have married you." Patrick's tone was flat.

She looked at him. "I understand that now."

"So forget him."

"Well, of course I will. But, Patrick, it was only *today* that all this happened. It will take me a little while to put it all behind me."

His voice was gruff. "Let's just get this clear. You'll be my wife. You won't be hanging around with Marcus Shelby anymore."

"I understand, Patrick."

"Good. Go on."

She made herself speak brightly. "So it turned out that Marcus didn't want marriage. And then, there you were. And you were so..."

He was smiling again. "Convincing?"

She looked shyly down and then back up. "Yes. You were *convincing*. Very. So I agreed to marry you. And..." She shrugged, her hands out. "Here I am."

He gave her a warm look. "I'm glad."

"Me, too." She waited, sure he was going to start explaining his own motives. But he said nothing. So she prompted, "Now, what about you?"

He pointed out the window. "Here comes the turn to Highway 20."

"Yes, I see. Now, what about you?"

He put his hand on her knee.

"Patrick?"

"Nice," he said softly, rubbing her knee. He gazed out the windshield, presumably looking for the turnoff, which Regina knew was clearly marked and just about impossible to miss.

"Patrick..."

He went on gently caressing her knee. She realized vaguely that her skin seemed to come more alive when he touched her. Her mind, on the other hand, seemed to go a little dim.

"Patrick, you were going to explain to me about... um..."

His hand slid up her thigh a little. "I better watch it, huh? We could become a road hazard."

"Um...yes. Yes, you should be careful...."

He caressed her thigh for a few moments more, during which time she completely forgot about what she'd been trying to get him to tell her. Then, when she knew she was going to have to remind him that driving was a serious responsibility, he reluctantly took his hand away.

She wasted ten minutes staring dreamily out the window smiling like a lovesick fool, before she remembered her intention to find out why he had proposed to her. She straightened in her seat and tried again.

He smiled and agreed to tell her—and then somehow he didn't.

It was like that for the entire trip. She'd bring the subject around where she wanted it. And then he would find a way to change it once more. When they pulled up to the valet parking area in front of one of the best casino/hotels in

South Shore, she knew no more about what he was really up to than she'd known when the drive started.

They were checked into their suite by eight-thirty.

The suite, newly remodeled they were told, had been designed with honeymooners in mind. It boasted a small terrace with a view of the lake, a huge round bed on a dais and a sitting room with a full bar. Each room seemed to flow into the next one, so that the bedroom was only separated from the sitting room by a wide arch. The bath, with its huge sunken tub, was also fully open to the bedroom. Only the room with the commode in it had a privacy door.

On the black marble counter of the bar, there was a huge fruit basket, as well as a silver ice bucket with a champagne bottle sticking out of it.

The bellman offered to open the champagne.

"We'll handle it," Patrick said, and tipped him.

Once the bellman had left, Regina stood on the pricey close-woven pale carpet and worried about the expense.

Patrick had just bought a house. He'd owned the North Magdalene Garage for under a year. She did not believe that he was wealthy. He couldn't possibly have money to throw around. And yet here he was, going all out to make their short honeymoon a time to remember.

Well—she squared her shoulders—she *did* have money. In fact, now she thought about it, maybe she'd hit on his real reason for wanting to marry her. Perhaps he wanted her as his bride because he was having money problems and knew that she was well-off.

The idea that he might be marrying her for her money wasn't a particularly pleasant one. But if it were true, then it was best if they could talk about his financial situation honestly.

She resolved that they really did have to talk frankly about all this soon. But for right now, she decided, this was going to be her honeymoon, too. And since she was sure she had more money than he did, she would pay for it.

She told him as much.

He shook his head. "Hell, no. This is on the old man anyway."

"The old man?"

"Yeah. My dad. Oggie."

"Oh. Yes. Oggie." It suddenly occurred to her that peculiar old Oggie Jones would very soon be her father-in-law. She felt a little shiver, remembering the way he had caught her watching Patrick that first day, and then how he had hobbled past the blanket at the picnic today, right before Marcus finally told her that he never intended to be a married man.

"This whole trip is a wedding present from him," Patrick continued on the subject of Oggie. "And don't worry about him being able to afford it. My dad is doing okay, when it comes to money."

"He certainly doesn't flaunt his wealth," she remarked delicately, thinking of old Oggie's threadbare shirts, baggy trousers and frayed suspenders.

Patrick chuckled at that. "Gina, you're something." He reached for her and pulled her against him. "Really something..." He bent his head and nibbled her lip.

She sighed.

He deepened the kiss. His tongue urged her lips to part, and his hands roamed her back. He raised his head, but only long enough to slant his lips the other way, and then he was kissing her again.

Her knees went all wobbly. But somehow she managed to get them to hold her up as he maneuvered her across the room and up the steps of the dais to the perimeter of the massive round bed. He sat, pulling her down with him. Then he urged her to stretch out, after which he slid over so that she was beneath him.

He kissed her some more. She wrapped her arms around his neck and kissed him right back.

And then he lifted his head enough to smile down at her.

"Your eyes are dark as storm clouds," he teased in a husky whisper.

She made a little mindless sound, raising a hand that felt deliciously heavy to trace the shape of his ear.

"I should feed you," he said.

She only smiled. He'd been kissing her, after all. And when he kissed her, she couldn't think anyway. She became a very stupid woman when he kissed her. Blissfully stupid.

"But I think first," he went on, "we should get ourselves a license and then find a wedding chapel."

A few of her wits returned. "We're getting married *tonight?*"

"Yep. Right away."

They made it to the Douglas County Clerk's office just before it closed at ten that night. Then, license in hand, they looked in the phone book and found a chapel.

It was called Millie and Everet's Chapel of Love in the Pines, though most of the pines in the immediate vicinity had long since been mowed down to make room for the big supermarket next door. There were two couples ahead of them, but Regina and Patrick had their turn at last.

At a few minutes before one on the morning of the Fourth of July, Regina Black became Mrs. Patrick Jones. When they left the Chapel of Love in the Pines, there were fireworks going off far out over the lake.

They returned to their suite at the hotel, opened the champagne and raided the fruit basket. Somehow, dinner had been skipped over in the process of accomplishing their marriage.

After consuming two glasses of champagne, a banana and a kiwifruit that Patrick had peeled and sectioned for her, Regina kicked off her shoes and slid up to rest among the huge pile of pillows on the giant bed. Once thoroughly comfortable, she admired her engagement diamond and wedding band and wondered where Patrick had acquired them.

She'd been completely surprised when he pulled them from his pocket in the wedding chapel. They were old, she knew. There were a few scratches on the bands and the diamonds were cut differently than more modern rings.

Regina didn't realize Patrick was watching her until he remarked, "You like your rings."

She looked up. She knew her face was soft and full of telltale emotions, but she didn't mind. Patrick was her husband now. A husband had a right to see his wife in her more tender moments.

"Oh, yes." She sighed. "They're so beautiful."

"They were my mother's wedding rings."

Regina mused on that. On the thought that she wore the rings that had sealed the vows of Oggie and Bathsheba Jones.

Patrick said, "My dad gave them to me just before I came to pick you up. I hope you don't mind that they're not new."

"Oh, Patrick. No, I don't mind. I don't mind at all. It's an honor."

Patrick chuckled.

Regina insisted, "No, I mean it. And if I were superstitious, I'd say that any marriage sealed with these rings was bound to last."

He laughed out loud at that, then grew more serious. "And why is that?"

"Well, whatever anyone in North Magdalene thinks of Oggie Jones, we all know how much he and your mother loved each other."

"You do, huh?" Patrick's expression was hard to read. She thought he looked indulgent, so she decided to go on.

"Yes." She nodded. "Absolutely. It's . . . well, it's like a beautiful romantic novel. How Oggie wandered into town, a footloose gambling man without a cent to his name, took one look at beautiful Bathsheba Riley and swore to marry her, even though everyone always assumed Bathsheba would marry rich Rory Drury."

"Things don't always turn out the way everyone expects," Patrick said.

"They certainly don't," Regina agreed. "They say Rory was terribly jealous."

"Yeah, that's what they say."

"They say he got his buddies together and beat Oggie up, left him battered and broken behind the Hole in the Wall, warning him to leave town if he knew what was good for him."

Misty-eyed, Regina looked down at her rings. Slowly, lovingly, she twisted them on her finger. She was lost in the tale, one of the legends of her town.

"But Oggie wouldn't do that," she continued. "Oh, no. He staggered inside and challenged Rory to a poker game. Of course, Rory couldn't back down and keep his pride. And Oggie, even badly injured and weak from loss of blood, won that game anyway. Won five thousand dollars from Rory, which in those days was enough to buy the Hole in the Wall from Stinky Collins. And Oggie did buy it, and proposed formally to Bathsheba, who said yes. And everything looked like it would work out beautifully for them. But then—"

"Hey." Patrick's teasing voice reached her, even through the magic of the old story.

She looked at him and smiled sheepishly. "I got carried away."

He shrugged. "It's a great story. But believe me, I've heard it already."

"I imagine so."

He was standing by the arch to the sitting room. "Come here." His voice had gone velvety.

She knew what was coming. She could see it in his eyes. On the drive back to the hotel, she'd been thinking that they would have a nice little talk when they got here. She'd imagined he'd be more willing to open up to her about his motives, now that the big step had been taken and they were husband and wife.

Gingerly she suggested, "Patrick, I had hoped we could talk for a while."

He shook his head. "Uh-uh. Not now. Now I want to make love. With my wife."

"But, Patrick, I—"

"Uh-uh. Come here."

She looked at him for a long moment, her desire fighting her good sense.

"Gina." The sound of the nickname he seemed to have coined for her was tender, but still there was command in it.

Still doubtful, but unable to resist him, she slid off the bed. Once upright, she smoothed the airy folds of her pale orchid chiffon dress, which she had bought two years ago and never worn.

Until tonight, her wedding night.

"Come here." This time he only mouthed the words.

She started down the steps of the dais, just as he began walking toward her. They met in the middle of the huge, opulent room.

He took her chin and tipped it up. "My old man always said that the right wife is everything." His fingers strayed over her jawline, into her loose hair. "I think I'm beginning to understand just what the hell he meant."

His mouth closed over hers. She sighed in delight. Sustaining the searing kiss, he walked her backward to the dais, up the short steps and to the bed.

Then he lifted his head. His eyes were like the sky, when it darkens to nighttime. There were shadows and secrets there, mystery and promise.

She thought of primitive rituals, ancient customs. A man took a woman for his wife. He promised to care for her and she for him. But then, after the ceremony that pronounced them wed, he must take her to bed and enter her body to make the vows binding.

And that was what Patrick was about to do now, Regina could see in the twilight shadows of his eyes. He would make love to his wife, the ultimate sealing of the vows they had made.

Into her mind once more crept all the things they hadn't said, everything he had yet to explain—why he had followed her up Sweetbriar Summit and laid her down in the meadow there, his reasons for demanding that she become his bride.

She understood exactly what he was doing now. He was sealing the promise they had made to each other as thoroughly as he could before she forced him to tell her what was in his mind and heart.

If he ever did tell her what was in his mind and heart....

"Patrick. We should talk."

He shook his head.

"But I—"

"Not now, Gina. Not tonight. Tonight is for touching and feeling. Not for talk."

Slowly, never letting go of her gaze, he raised both hands and placed his palms flat against the delicate swells of her breasts. She gasped. Her nipples, beneath her clothing, rose and hardened with stunning eagerness into the center of his palms.

He rubbed, keeping his palms flat. "Ah, yeah..." It was a whispered sigh.

Regina sighed, too. And as the sigh floated from her lips, she finally truly accepted that she would get no answers from him tonight. She wanted the pleasure his touch gave. She craved it. Everything else was slowly fading to nothing. There was Patrick and his kiss, his touch, his body that called to her body. Nothing else mattered. Not for tonight.

He went on brushing her breasts with his palms, causing tiny agonies of pleasure to pulse from the tightened buds of her nipples through every inch of her. Down in the cove between her thighs, she could feel the throbbing, the moisture. Her body wept for need of him.

Her dress had a deep V-neck, the layers of chiffon overlapping and gathered at the waist. His thumbs found the slit of the V and slowly parted it, until he could guide the dress from her shoulders.

Regina blinked and swayed and then realized that the top half of her dress was down to her waist. There was a knowing smile on his mouth. He lowered his head and kissed her lips again, a tender, brushing kiss that aroused her utterly with its very restraint. And as he kissed her, his hands gently, relentlessly went about their business, taking her slip to her waist and unhooking her bra.

When he lifted his head to look in her eyes again, she realized she was nude to the waist.

"Oh!" she said, surprised.

He chuckled, then cupped both of her small breasts in his big hands. "So pretty," he muttered.

"They're not—I mean, I'm not...." She was blushing furiously. She made herself finish. "I'm not very big...."

He flicked her nipples with his thumbs. She groaned. "I know," he said. He didn't seem to mind that she was small-breasted, not at all.

"But I thought most men..."

He chuckled again. "You women. You get some idea in your head about what all men like. All men are different. Some like big breasts. And some..." He lowered his head and licked one erect, aching nipple. Regina moaned. He blew where he'd licked. "Some men like small, high breasts. And some men don't give a damn about breasts. They like long legs, or tiny waists or..." He licked and blew on the other breast.

On a groan, Regina implored, "Or what?"

"Or the whole picture." He took her nipple in his mouth.

She clutched his head and held him against her and felt the way his tongue swirled around, making her crazy, making her moan.

At last he lifted his head. After drawing in a shuddering breath, she dared to ask, "What do you mean, the whole picture?"

He put his hands at her waist and began smoothing her filmy dress and the slip beneath it down over her hips. "The whole picture. The whole woman. Put your hand on my shoulder." He knelt, and lifted her feet, one then the other, getting the dress and slip clear and away. He then tossed them quite cavalierly onto the big bed. He took her panty hose and her panties and whisked them down, off and away, just as he had the dress and slip.

She was naked before him, and aroused enough that it took her a moment to try to cover herself with her hands.

"Uh-uh. No, you don't." He took her wrists and held them away from her body. And he looked at her.

Embarrassment stained every inch of her bared skin pink. "Oh, Patrick, I . . ."

"The whole woman," he murmured. "Yeah, I'm a *whole woman* sort of guy." He went on looking, while, above the wrists he was gripping, her hands became fists. She tipped her head toward the ceiling and pressed her eyes closed.

She wondered, not even knowing that she was whimpering a little, how a person could feel both aroused and thoroughly mortified at the same time.

He said softly, "Gina, I'm telling you I like the way you look. The way *all* of you looks. The way all the parts of you...fit together." He let go of one wrist. She waited, not daring to open her eyes.

And then she felt it. The pads of his fingers brushed the side swell of one breast.

"I like this," he hoarsely whispered. "And this." He palmed her waist, pressing his thumb into her navel as her belly contracted. "And this." A finger trailed over the swell of her hip, leaving goose bumps in its wake. "Are you listening to me, Gina?"

She bit her lip and managed to nod.

"Good." His hand slid around and cupped the swell of her bottom. She groaned. "And I like the way you do that."

"Um. What?"

"The way you groan. Like you're really too much of a lady to groan, but you can't help yourself. You groan anyway. I like that. It gets me hot."

His hand slid back to the front of her then. She groaned some more as he found the heart of her, as he parted her with his fingers and began to stroke her as he had a lifetime ago—only that afternoon—up on Sweetbriar Summit beneath the burning sun.

"I like the way your body moves for me." In and out, slowly, deliciously, his fingers worked their magic. "I like the way your white skin goes pink and your nipples stand up, like they're begging for me to kiss them." Just as he said that, he bent his head and covered one breast with his mouth. He stroked her with his hand and he laved her nipple with his tongue.

Regina knew she was going to die of delight. But she didn't die. She'd never been so alive, as she brazenly writhed and moaned in response to the touch of Patrick Jones. He stroked her faster in answer to the quickening movement of her hips and she rode his hand until she felt herself going over the edge.

"Yeah," he breathed against her breast. "Yeah, Gina. Oh, yeah..."

There was an explosion of light behind her lids, as her body contracted around his wonderful fingers. She whimpered and sobbed and sank slowly to the curved edge of the mattress. She was aware of his strong arm, gently helping her down.

Then for a measureless time she knew nothing but the waves of pleasure that pulsed and receded and then pulsed once again. She drew in long, hungry breaths as Patrick continued to stroke her, extending the pleasure, drawing it out into eternity and at the same time easing her way back to the world.

A few minutes later, when reality returned, she found that she was sitting on the side of the bed, gripping fistfuls of the bedspread in each hand. Patrick, silent, waiting, had straightened again and was standing before her.

"Open your eyes, Gina. Look at me. Won't you, please?"

She might have resisted a command, but never such a tender, needful plea. Her eyes fluttered open. Her bent head slowly lifted. She looked up his fully clothed body to meet his waiting eyes.

"Touch me." The words were hoarse, husky.

Regina stared at him, knowing what he meant. Her throat was dry. And the rest of her body felt so heavy and hot—ripe with sex and satiation and now, once more, a desire that seemed to bloom right on top of complete fulfillment. His request had excited her even more than it shocked her.

Quickly he shrugged out of his shirt and tossed it aside. His beautiful chest and hard stomach excited her. His eyes encouraged her, beseeched her.

"Come on. Touch me."

She lifted a hesitant hand. And shyly set it upon him. Though his clothing was between that touch and his manhood, his body jerked. He stifled a moan.

Her senses swam at the hard, marvelous feel of him beneath her hand. And the way he responded to her reticent touch. There was power here, for her, in what she might do to him, give to him. The same power as he had just held over her.

Her heart beat faster. Desire, curiosity... and awe, too. They were all there, overriding her shyness, and her confusion at the newness of all of this. Here, after all, was glory and splendor, wonder and fulfillment.

For her—and for him.

There was a button on his waistband. She slid it from its hole. She found the zipper tab and pulled it down. The two sides of his slacks parted. She guided them down, helped him slide off his soft leather shoes and get rid of his socks, just as he had helped her to remove her clothes. She straightened again to tenderly pull his briefs away, careful that they didn't catch on his hardness. At last he was as naked as she.

A little of her shyness returned. It showed in her renewed hesitancy as she once more raised her hand and touched his arousal with diffident fingertips.

He gasped.

She dared to stroke him, just with her fingertips. She found him silky and hot. He was so strong, both in his lean, powerful body and in his will that had chosen her and pursued her and claimed her as his within a span of weeks. So very strong. And yet he moaned and jerked just from the light touch of her hand.

Cautiously, experimentally, she wrapped her hand around his hardness. She tried one lingering stroke, sliding her curled fingers smoothly up and down the satin length of him.

"Oh, man..." Patrick gritted out. "I...think that'll do it...."

And then everything happened at once.

He pushed her firmly back on the bed, urging her to scoot up and around until she could lie with her head upon the mountain of pillows. Then he nudged her thighs apart with one of his own and loomed above her. She looked up into his flushed face, his burning eyes.

She felt bewildered. "Patrick? Did I...do it wrong?"

He let out a pained chuckle. "Wrong? Hell, no. You did it right. Just right."

"I did?"

"Yeah, you did."

She could feel him, there, at her entrance. And then, very gently, he began to push himself inside. She watched his face, her shyness once more forgotten, and she saw that it was almost painful for him to go so slowly, to so carefully restrain himself.

"Am I hurting you?" He seemed to moan the words.

She shook her head against the tumbled pillows. Though she had felt some sensitivity down there all evening, now it didn't hurt at all. She was too relaxed. And too aroused.

"Good." He pressed home.

She moaned as she fully received him.

Then he levered up on his arms and, joined with her, he met her eyes. "Wrap your legs around me."

A little awkwardly, but with complete willingness, she did as he asked.

"This time," he said, "you're coming with me."

And then he started to move—slowly at first, and then faster, and then slowly again. Regina clung to him, moving with him, catching his rhythms, giving them back, adding rhythms of her own.

Her mind spun away. She was pure feeling, a living shimmer of sensation, as she learned what it was to climb to the stars and to hover there, looking into her husband's face until he cried aloud and soared off the edge of the world.

She watched him, her own eyes widening, her breath catching on a joyful sob as she found she was joining him, winging toward heaven right along with him.

They spun out, together, into a universe of bursting stars.

He allowed her to rest for a while. But not too long. Soon enough, it started all over again.

Though the warm weight across her midsection made it difficult, Regina rolled over and squinted at the clock radio by the bed.

She groaned. It was well past noon.

She turned her head—and found herself looking into Patrick's slumbering face.

My sweet Lord. It had not been a dream. Last night—or early this morning, rather—she had married Patrick Jones. It was his arm across her stomach, his hairy thigh pressed against her leg.

He had followed her up Sweetbriar Summit and he'd made love to her there, beneath the sky. And he'd made her agree to marry him. He'd swept her off to Tahoe. And she *had* married him. Then they'd returned here, to their hotel suite.

She'd tried to talk to him. But he hadn't wanted to talk. Instead, they'd made love some more.

Much more.

Images of the things they'd done flashed through her brain, causing an agonized flush that started at her toes and then seemed to flood every square inch of her unclothed body. She had reveled in every caress.

But somehow, now that it was the morning after, she was shocked at the way she had behaved. And she really should have insisted that he explain a few things before she... performed all of those appallingly intimate acts with him.

"'Morning." Patrick's eyes were open. He was smiling at her.

"Morning is already gone," she informed him primly.

His smile deepened, crinkling the corners of his eyes. "Yes, ma'am. So it is." He brought his sleep-flushed face close to hers and kissed her on the mouth.

Then he sat and stretched enthusiastically, not caring a bit when the sheet slid away to display his most private parts. Regina sat up herself, modestly clutching the sheet and significantly looking away from what he so shamelessly revealed.

"Hey," he said, and tapped her on the shoulder.

"What?"

"Don't get prissy."

"I'm sure I have no idea what you're talking about."

"When you get prissy, I get determined to make you hot."

"That's ridiculous."

"Oh, is it?" Apparently deciding he had a point to prove, he nibbled where he'd tapped. Pleasurable little waves of sensation rippled out from where he nibbled. Regina bit her lip, clutched the sheet and tried not to sigh. She really had to remember her goal to get him to talk.

"Patrick?"

"Hmm?"

"We should order breakfast." She did her absolute best to sound like a person who would brook no nonsense. She didn't succeed too well.

He went on nibbling, up over her shoulder and across the wing of her collarbone. "Maybe I'll just have *you,* à la carte."

"Patrick..."

"No fruit juice. No toast. No coffee. Just the main course." He started sucking right where he'd already left a mark.

She wriggled and stiffened beneath the wonderful things his mouth was doing to her. She knew she should pull away, but somehow she wasn't pulling away. "Patrick, I haven't eaten anything but two pieces of fruit and some champagne since lunch yesterday." She tried to sound chastening, but her voice came out petulant.

"Sorry, baby. We'll order room service."

"I am not a baby." It was an outright reprimand.

That did it. His lips ceased their tender torment. He lifted his head and took her shoulders and turned her so that she was facing him amid the tumble of bedclothes and pillows.

"Okay, what's going on?"

Now that he wasn't distracting her, she found it very easy to be specific. "I want to *talk.* I mean it. I've married you, just as you wanted. And you know all about why I did it. I, on the other hand, don't have a clue as to what you're after. Since we got in your Bronco yesterday evening, I've tried in a thousand different tactful ways to get you to explain what you're up to. Because I *will* have honesty, above all, in this marriage. But being tactful apparently doesn't work with you. So I'm through being tactful. I want to know why you married me. Now."

He raked his tangled hair back and rubbed his eyes.

"I mean it, Patrick."

"Okay," he growled.

"You said okay before and then you told me nothing."

His eyes flashed. "Well, I'm saying *okay* again. And this time I'll tell you whatever the hell you want to know."

"Oh, you will, will you?"

"Yes. I will. Just ask. And I'll answer."

"Fine." She held her head high. "What I want to know first is . . ." Oh, this was difficult to say.

"I can't answer if you don't have the guts to ask."

"I have the guts."

"Then do it."

"Fine." She dragged in a determined breath. "Did you marry me for my money?"

Chapter Nine

A slow smile curved Patrick's mouth. "Is it a lot of money?"

Regina kept her head high. He was not going to see how much it hurt to think that he only wanted her for her money. "It's enough that I never have to work if I don't want to."

"Hmm." He tugged on the sheet a little and seemed to turn that bit of information over in his mind. "A rich wife. The dream of every sensible man."

"I'm not rich." She looked at his hair, which was sticking up in all directions, and at the sleep wrinkles on his face, and she wondered how he could be so handsome. She told herself it didn't matter that this conversation was breaking her heart. The bitter truth was always preferable to a fool's illusion.

"If you're not rich, what are you?" he asked.

"I'm . . . well, I suppose you could say I'm well-to-do."

"Hmm. Well-to-do, huh?"

She glared at him. "You said you'd answer. I haven't heard any answers, only more questions. Rather crass questions, actually."

He tipped his head, studying her. Then he said, very tenderly, "Gina. I'm sorry."

She looked away. "What does that mean?"

"It means you're right. I'm acting like a real creep. And I'm sorry."

She was determined not to be a fool. "What for? I asked you to be honest."

"Yeah, but I wasn't being honest."

"What are you saying?"

"I'm saying I was mad."

"Why?"

"Because you wouldn't make love with me. I wanted to get even with you."

"I don't understand."

His eyes were tender. "You really don't, do you?" There was a kind of gentle awe in his voice. "You don't know a damn thing about the rotten games that can be played between a woman and a man."

She didn't know how to reply. And she was wondering what kind of "rotten games" he had played with other women—but then she decided she'd just as soon not know. "Well, I . . . I'm not terribly experienced with men. I know that."

Now his eyes gleamed. "You're doing just fine."

She blushed. "Well, thanks."

"Look—" his tone was serious again "—I don't want you for your money. We can live on what I make, I promise you. Why don't you just get a lawyer to draw up an agreement that says I can't put my greedy hands on anything that belongs to you? I'll sign it."

She was silent for a moment. Then, "You really mean that, don't you?"

His expression was utterly serious. "I do."

It was her turn to tug on the sheet. She believed him—and felt relief to know that the money wasn't the reason. She also felt petty and small. "No. Of course, I wouldn't do that. You're my *husband* and I . . . I . . ."

He reached out and pulled her against him. "Easy, Gina. It's okay." He slowly stroked her hair.

"I just . . . I want to know . . ."

"What?"

"Why? Why did you marry me?" Before he could answer, she slipped from his embrace and blurted out her *real* question, the question she had never imagined in her wildest dreams she would ever dare to ask him. "You don't . . . *love* me, after all. Do you?"

For a long time he only stared at her, while she waited in an agony of embarrassment over what she'd just presumed to say.

Finally she could bear the silence no longer. "Well?"

"Gina . . ."

"Please. Just tell me."

He pried one of her hands free of the sheet and kissed it, then enclosed it between both of his. "I need a wife."

She pulled her hand from his gentle clasp and pushed her hair from her eyes. "You what?"

"I need a wife. For when my girls come home."

"But—"

He went on before she could finish. "Look, I want to make a home for them. A real home."

"But Patrick, they live with Marybeth. In Arkansas." She repeated the obvious, because she had yet really to comprehend what he was getting at.

"They live with their mother right now. But they miss their home, and all their friends. Until last year, neither of them had ever lived anywhere else but North Magdalene."

"But you can't expect Marybeth to just—"

He put up a hand. "I know Marybeth. I was married to her for eight years. She'll bring Marnie and Teresa to me eventually, when she finally feels bad enough about keeping them so far away from their home. *And* when she finally accepts the fact that she's taken on too much for one person to accomplish alone. The woman is trying to build a real-estate business single-handedly. And she's been neglecting the girls because she just plain doesn't have any time. I have a feeling she's getting close to the point where she's willing to let me have them for a while. I think she'll be turning them over to me sometime during the summer, when they won't have to worry about school."

"And then?"

"And then, since I have a decent place for them to live and you at my side, I'll be ready to suggest that she just let them live with me. Because if there's a perfect woman to be my wife and the mother of my daughters, it's you, Gina."

He watched her, his eyes as bright and intense as when he was making love to her. He seemed to be willing her to understand. "I'm no big winner in life, you know? Teresa and Marnie are the only things I've done that make sense. And I want to do more for them than getting the support check in the mail on schedule every month. I don't want them growing up thinking their father doesn't give a damn, even though that's probably what they've thought up until now, because I have not been the most dedicated father in the world.

"But damn it, a man can change. And I'm working on that, on changing. I want to show them how much I love them and how much it means to me that they're in the world. To do that, I need time with them, day-to-day time, so they'll know they can count on me. Can you understand that?''

Regina swallowed, because there was a lump in her throat. She knew she probably ought to be angry at him, for sweeping her off her feet instead of telling her this simple, heart-rending truth.

But she was not angry with him. Not in the least.

Beneath the corner of one of the pillows, she caught sight of her slip, which Patrick had carelessly tossed on the bed when he undressed her the night before. She pulled it free of the tangled blankets and tugged it on over her head, smoothing it hastily into place beneath the sheet.

''Gina?'' He sounded very worried.

She asked, ''Why didn't you just tell me that? Instead of—''

''Seducing you?'' He chuckled, but it was not a relaxed sound.

''Yes.''

''Because I...'' For once, he was the one at a loss for words.

''Go on.''

''All right. Because I thought you'd turn me down, if I laid it all out for you.''

She looked at him, thinking of all that had happened on Sweetbriar Summit and then trying to imagine it another way. Trying to picture Patrick telling her of his daughters instead of making love to her. What would her answer have been? She couldn't be completely sure.

''I think you should have been honest,'' she hedged.

''But if I had, would you be my wife this morning?''

''I would have respected your honesty.''

He made a knowing sound in his throat. "Right. You would have respected my honesty—and said no."

She was silent. He did have a point. In appealing to her starved senses, he'd held her in thrall. It would have been quite possible, had his arguments been calm and rational, for her to have simply said no.

Patrick was watching her closely. His scrutiny made her uneasy.

All at once, unable to be still, she rose from the bed and went to the glass door that led out onto the terrace. Outside, it was a crystal-clear day. The sun shimmered on the lake. There were a few small powerboats and several sailboarders in sight.

"Damn it, Gina." His voice, from behind her, was low and rough. "What the hell are you thinking?"

She faced him again, met his wary gaze. But she didn't answer him.

"Gina."

She said nothing. She knew she was tormenting him. And, though she was a kind woman at heart, she wanted to torture him right then. She had a right to, at least for the few more seconds it took her to accept how skillfully he'd avoided answering her question about love.

She found herself wondering about Chloe Swan. Before he married Marybeth, everyone in town had been sure that he'd found his true love in Chloe. And almost everyone in North Magdalene believed that Chloe had never stopped loving him. They said that Patrick had been upset when Chloe ran off last year. Could it be that Patrick still loved her, as everyone thought she loved him?

Not that it mattered, Regina chided herself. Her speculations were all based on hearsay and rumor. And Chloe had been gone for a year now. It was a distinct possibility that she would never return. Surely, whatever was between Patrick and Chloe was now firmly in the past.

Patrick rose from the bed. "Damn it. What the hell is it? Are you thinking you're going to divorce me now? Is that it?" He strode toward her across their hotel suite, magnificently naked and completely unashamed.

And that was when it hit her.

She was in love with him.

It was quite obvious that he did not love her, yet her heart was his. She had planned a quiet, happy life for herself with a shy, unassuming man. And ended up eloping with one of the Jones boys.

It was crazy. Regina was terrified.

And yet she felt absolutely wonderful.

As she had learned yesterday, naked in the sun on Sweetbriar Summit, her life was no longer sane and uneventful. She loved Patrick Jones.

And not only that; she had gone and *married* him.

It had been a bold, gutsy act. She was downright proud of herself.

He reached her, shoved his fingers through her hair and lifted her face so that her mouth was just inches below his. "Don't you dare tell me you want a divorce."

She shook her head, as much as she could with his hands holding her still. She loved him, and if she had anything to say about it, they would make this marriage work.

"No, Patrick. I don't want a divorce."

He let out a relieved sigh. His insistent hands gentled in her hair. "Good. Now lighten up. Things could be worse...." His mouth met hers.

"Patrick," she breathed against his lips, "I really am hungry."

"We'll order breakfast soon. I promise. Soon..."

* * *

They remained at Lake Tahoe for three more days. Regina had the time of her life. Like a late-blooming flower, she basked in the sun of the love that had found her at last.

They went boating and Regina tried waterskiing. They took in more than one show. They ate in fine restaurants where the crystal gleamed in candlelight and beyond huge banks of windows the lake glimmered beneath the moon. They stayed up sinfully late and slept until lunchtime.

And they made love. Frequently and fulfillingly. Regina relished every moment of it.

But on Wednesday, it was time to go home.

They arrived in North Magdalene at a little after one in the afternoon. Patrick carried her across the threshold of his house, shoving the door shut behind them with his boot. He kissed her long and thoroughly.

Then he set her down and went out to the Bronco to bring in their bags. After the truck was unloaded, he handed her a set of keys to his house and his vehicle, then headed on foot to the garage to see how his business had fared in his absence.

Regina wandered the rooms of her husband's house for a few moments, thinking with some anticipation that she certainly had a lot to do.

Next, she returned to her house next door, where she discovered everything was just as she had left it, except for the blinking light on her answering machine, which she decided not to deal with right then.

She swiftly changed into old jeans, tennis shoes and a worn shirt and poured herself a glass of juice with ice. After that, she ran up the window shades to let in some light and found a tablet and pencil. She went through the rooms of the house she'd grown up in, making herself a list of what she wanted to keep and what she would dispose of.

The doorbell rang precisely twenty-nine minutes after she had entered the house. Through the lace panels over the front windows, she could see who it was.

Nellie.

Regina didn't even consider not answering. Nellie, like everyone else in North Magdalene, would have to be dealt with. There was no sense putting off the inevitable. Still carrying her pad and pencil, Regina marched to her front door and pulled it back.

Nellie gave a little gasp. And then she swiftly scanned Regina's stubbornly smiling face.

"Hello, Nellie."

"So." Nellie made a nasal sound, a disapproving *harumph*. "It's true, isn't it?" Her small eyes glittered with unspoken accusations.

"What's true, Nellie?"

"You have eloped with Patrick Jones."

"Yes, it's true."

"Oh, my sweet Lord in heaven, what would your dear mother say?"

"The question is moot, Nellie. My mother is dead."

Nellie blinked a few times and did some sputtering.

Regina politely inquired, "Would you like to come in for a few minutes? I could pour you some juice." Nellie's lips began twitching in wounded outrage. Regina blithely continued, "But it's only fair to warn you, I really don't have much time to visit. Patrick and I have decided we'll live at his house and rent this one, and there are a million things to do. But I could spare a minute or two for you."

Nellie didn't want to talk about how long she'd stay yet. She wanted to express how deeply she'd been abused. "I came by Sunday morning. You were gone." Her voice quivered with hurt. "I was worried sick about you. And then I went to church to find Tondalaya Clark playing the hymns. I learned you'd asked Delilah to find someone to take your place. You asked *Delilah,* when you could just as well have asked me. I was crushed."

"I'm sorry, Nellie. I honestly am. But I simply was not ready, when I talked to you Saturday, to explain what was going on in my private life."

"I thought you were my friend."

"I *am* your friend."

"You don't trust me."

"Yes, I do. I would trust you with my life."

"But not with your secrets."

"Well, now, Nellie. You're not very good at keeping secrets. And we both know that."

Nellie actually looked as if she might cry. "Oh, this is horrible. It's just like when Delilah ran off with that wild man, Sam Fletcher. She told me nothing, though I was her closest friend. And now you have done the same thing. Gone and eloped with Patrick Jones without a single word to me about it. Tell the truth. You knew that you were leaving with him when I caught you at your car Saturday and you told me that you and Marcus had broken up. You knew then. Didn't you?"

Regina answered very gently. "Yes. I knew then."

Nellie pressed her lips together, folded her thin arms over her flat chest and looked away. "Well," she harumphed.

"Nellie, are you coming in or not?"

"I—"

"If not, I really want to get back to the job I was doing."

"You have hurt me deeply."

"Nellie."

"All right." Nellie sniffed. "I'll come in so that you may properly apologize to me."

Nellie stayed for nearly an hour. By the time she finally got up to leave, she was still convinced that Regina had made a grave and irreparable error in throwing over the warm and wonderful Marcus Shelby for a troublemaking roughneck like Patrick Jones.

However, Nellie had decided to forgive Regina for not confiding in her. With a Jones for a husband, Regina would be needing a sympathetic ear. And Nellie, never one to hold a grudge, would be available anytime.

That night, Patrick came home a little before six to find the dining room table set with his wife's dishes.

"Already moving things around, I see." There was both pride and approval in his voice. They were in the kitchen and he backed her up against the sink, using only his body, since his hands were stained with the evidence that he'd done more than hang around the office at the garage. He'd also been helping his two mechanics.

"I've been very busy." She kissed him on his chin, right on a smear of engine oil. "And you need a shower."

"Take one with me."

"Not possible. I have to finish dinner."

"Dinner can wait. I can't."

"Patrick..."

"Mmm. I love how you taste. So sweet."

"Patrick. The dinner..."

"Always worried about food."

"We have to eat...."

"Mmm... Soon. I promise. Soon..."

The roast ended up a little overdone, but Patrick didn't complain.

After dinner, they called Marybeth and the girls in Arkansas, to tell them about the marriage. It was a brief and rather awkward conversation. Marybeth sounded quite stunned, but did murmur that she wished them well. Teresa, the older girl, got on the line and told both Regina and her father in a stilted voice that she had always "admired Regina's good works," and was "very happy for them." Marnie could not be coaxed to take the phone.

When they hung up, Regina told herself that the important thing was that the girls now knew they had a stepmother. Of course, it would take them time to accept the idea.

Patrick took her hand. "Come on. Let's get some air."

They went outside and jumped the fence to sit on her porch, since she had a swing. After a few minutes of idly swinging and not saying much, they started to talk of their plans.

"This weekend," he promised, "I'll move the swing to the other house."

She told him that she'd done some measuring and was now sure her window treatments would fit his windows, and that she wanted to replace some of his rather beat-up furniture with hers. Also, she wanted to paint several of the rooms. And to choose nicer furniture from the extra sets at her house for the girls' rooms.

"There's a nice oak set in the back bedroom that would probably be good. And when I was a girl, I had all white wicker in my room. It's still in the attic. Maybe one of the girls would like it. Of course, it would need repainting, but I can handle that."

"Wicker and oak for the girls." Patrick chuckled. "You really have been busy."

She leaned against him in the swing and he casually raised his arm and draped it across her shoulders. "Tell me what they're like," she prompted.

Since the morning Patrick told her that he wanted his daughters to live with them, she had been imagining what it might be like to have two children to care for. She was trying not to get starry-eyed over it. Of course there would be difficulties to overcome, if Patrick's prediction came true and Marybeth did let him have the girls. But they were difficulties Regina would embrace for the chance to have what for so long had passed her by: a real family of her own.

Patrick rested his chin against her hair. "You want to know what Teresa and Marnie are like?"

"Yes."

"Well, they're basically good kids. But they haven't had it easy, with all the problems their mother and I had."

Like what, specifically? Regina wanted to ask. But she didn't. She decided to simply let him talk for now and ask questions later. As she reminded herself lately whenever she became anxious about all she and Patrick had yet to learn about each other, they had their whole lives to do it. They didn't have to rush.

He went on. "Teresa's just turned twelve. She's big for her age and has her mother's hazel eyes. She's going through a religious phase."

"How so?"

"Well, when I went to see them in the spring, she was considering joining the Catholic church so that she could become a nun."

"I see."

His musing voice continued, explaining how Teresa seemed very serious for someone so young. And that Marnie, who was small and wiry at nine, was a hard kid to pin down. A tomboy, Marnie hated baths and dresses. "When I was there the last time, she wore the same pair of torn-up jeans the whole five days," he said. "Also, she can swear like a sailor. Her mother can't control her at all."

"Hmm." Regina rubbed her head against his shoulder, thinking that, from what he was telling her, it would be quite a challenge if the girls did come. Still, she couldn't suppress her growing anticipation. Having the girls with them was a challenge she would welcome, no matter how rough things got.

As they sat there idly swinging and talking, more than one of their neighbors just happened to stroll by. Greetings were exchanged and congratulations extended to the newlyweds. Both Patrick and Regina waved and smiled. They were careful to act totally unconcerned, though they knew that the eyes of the town were on them and would be for quite a while to come.

After dark came, Patrick whispered in her ear, "Think we've shown them all enough for one night?"

"Oh, I suppose." She twined her fingers more tightly with his. "But you know when we go in, they'll all be disappointed."

"No, they won't. They'll be able to imagine what we're doing. And that's much more exciting than having us in plain sight, holding hands like a couple of high school kids and swinging on a swing."

They got up, still holding hands, jumped the fence to the other house and went inside. What they did when they reached the bedroom was, in Regina's opinion, a thousand times more exciting than anyone was ever likely to imagine.

The next morning after Patrick left for the garage, Regina was just getting ready to call old Mrs. Leslie and offer to drop by for a few hours before lunch when the front door flew open.

"Where the hell is my new damn daughter-in-law?"

Oggie Jones had come to call.

He lowered his cane, which he'd used to shove the door open, and stomped into the house. "Regina? Regina, where are you, gal?"

Regina, already halfway down the hall from the dining room and kitchen, drew in a long breath and answered, "Right here . . . Father." She rushed to meet him.

He looked her up and down. "Father, eh?"

"Would you prefer I called you—"

He waved away the other possibilities before she could voice them. "Father's just dandy. Now be a good kid and get me some coffee." He hobbled right past her, headed for the kitchen.

"Be my guest," she muttered wryly to his retreating back.

He chortled, but didn't turn. "Don't mind if I do."

In the kitchen, after he'd poured a hypoglycemic's nightmare worth of sugar into his coffee, he hoisted his feet onto a spare chair and lit up a cigar. Regina, who did not approve of smoking, found she was not quite able, under the stare of those little black eyes, to ask him to extinguish the smelly thing. So she fumbled around in the cupboards until she found an ashtray, which she plunked down on the breakfast table beside him.

He glanced at it, then puffed for a moment. "I came to welcome you to the family."

"Well, that was thoughtful of you."

He waved his cigar. "Thoughtful, hell. We're always glad to get another classy broad." He flicked his ash. "Patrick treatin' you right?"

"Why, yes. He's treating me wonderfully."

"Good. If he doesn't, you come to me."

"Well, I—"

He waved his cigar. "Never mind, you don't have to say anything. I told you to come to me, so you know I'm available. We both know you'll never do any such thing. In fact, if you're like the rest of them, when you end up with some big problem, you'll mess everything up royally and I'll have to come in later and save the day. But at least you know I offered. And I meant it.''

"Oh, well, then. Of course.''

"I mean, since this was all my idea, I figure I should be at least a little responsible if there's any problems.''

"Pardon me? *Your* idea?''

"Aw, come on. You know it was my damn idea. I saw you watchin' my boy that first day he moved in. And that was when it come to me. Just like it did with my other three kids. I picked out Amy for Brendan and Sam for Delilah. And if you think gettin' Sam and Delilah together wasn't a job, you ain't thinkin'. I thought that was the roughest it could get. Until Jared and Eden. Then I realized I hadn't known what rough was.

"You, on the other hand, were a much easier project. It turned out you wanted a husband. And Patrick wanted a decent wife. And when I saw you lookin' at him that day, I realized you were the one for him. And about damn time, too. And now you two are hitched. Patrick, who only used to smile at a good joke, is grinnin' like an idiot all the time. And my vow is kept.''

"What vow?''

"Don't rush me, don't rush me. So how d'you like the rings?''

Regina, who was feeling a little dizzy at all she was hearing, managed to croak out, "I love them. Thank you. And for the honeymoon, too.''

"My pleasure. Purely my pleasure. Gimme a refill, gal, will ya?''

Regina got up and gave Oggie more coffee, after which he explained that on the deathbed of his beloved Bathsheba, he had vowed to see that each of his children found the perfect mate. A couple of his kids had had to try more than once.

But at last they'd all got it right. In heaven, his Bathsheba smiled all the time now.

"Well, that's just...lovely," Regina said, since she didn't know what else to say.

He cackled. "Think I'm bonkers, don't ya?"

"Ah...no. Of course not."

"You'll get used to me."

She imagined she'd have to. "Well, certainly," she said. "Of course I will."

Oggie smashed his cigar in the ashtray, hauled himself to his feet and leaned on his cane. "And now I'm outta here. You take care of my boy, and you and me will get along just fine. Don't bother to see me out. I know how to find the damn door."

"But I—"

"I mean it. Stay put."

"Well, all right. Good morning, then. Father."

Cackling, he hobbled out.

Regina stared after him. When she heard the door slam, she realized she was smiling.

To think she had found him frightening. Now she could see that, in his rough way, he was quite charming. And very dear. And it didn't bother her in the least that he'd had a hand in her marriage to Patrick. If anything, she was grateful.

In fact, as the first week of her marriage went by, Regina found that very little bothered her. Not her odd father-in-law, or the way people whispered about her in the street, or Nellie's never-ending tendency to drop by and warn her that she was heading for heartbreak.

For the first time in her life, she knew what happiness was: it was waking in the morning to find Patrick beside her, coming home from helping someone else to discover he'd dropped by for lunch or looking up from the book she was reading to meet his sapphire eyes.

Regina was in love. And even though her love was not returned, nothing could dim the joy she felt. Patrick proved every moment that he took being her husband seriously. He went to work every day and he came home on time every night. And in his arms she found heaven. Her life was just right. She had no complaints. Perhaps she was even a little smug in her happiness—which was probably why she acted so unwisely the day that Marcus Shelby came to call.

A week after she returned from her honeymoon, Regina came home from a three-hour stint as volunteer librarian at the community library to find Marcus sitting on the porch of the house where she used to live.

"Regina!" he called when he caught sight of her.

Regina hesitated, remembering that she'd promised Patrick on the day they married that she would stay away from Marcus.

Marcus stood and fussily brushed the wrinkles from his slacks. Looking at him, Regina wondered how she ever could have imagined spending her life with him. It had been a week and a half since the picnic in Sweetbriar Park. But to Regina, it seemed like years.

Marcus finished brushing at his slacks and started down the steps to meet her at the gate. She stood still and watched him approach, realizing that she felt absolutely nothing for him now beyond a sort of vague affection. She wondered if that was all she'd ever felt.

"Regina, I would like a private word with you." Marcus's expression was rather pinched.

Regina sighed. "Marcus, we really don't have anything to say to each other."

His narrow shoulders twitched as he drew himself up. "Regina, whatever you believe, I have cared for you deeply. That's why I must tell you a few things. *Someone* must tell you, and it might as well be me. I'll do it for the sake of all we once shared."

"Marcus, what *are* you talking about?"

His eyes scanned the pyracantha bushes by the front gate, as if he expected Nellie or someone equally nosy to be lurking there. "May we please go inside?"

"Marcus, I really—"

"Please." He looked very upset.

Again, Regina thought of her promise to Patrick. But somehow now, looking at Marcus, feeling nothing stronger than watered-down fondness, she could see no harm in being alone with him. And perhaps, after he got whatever was bothering him off his chest, his distress would fade. Poor Marcus. He simply didn't deal well with his own emotions at all.

"Please," he said again. "Just a few moments, I promise."

"Well, all right. Come on inside." She started for the other gate to the house she and Patrick now shared.

"Wait. Where are you going?"

She glanced back at him. "In the house."

"But that's *his* house."

"It's my house, too, Marcus. Patrick and I are married, remember?"

"But can't we just go in *your* house?"

"No." She was still a little uncomfortable about breaking her promise to Patrick, even though it was a thoroughly unnecessary promise. Somehow, to go with Marcus into the house she didn't even live in anymore felt way too much like sneaking around. "It's *our* house or nothing," she said, and went through the gate without pausing again.

Marcus stayed out on the sidewalk until Regina was almost to the porch. Then she heard him open the gate and hurry through.

Inside, she offered him a seat on the couch. He perched there gingerly.

"Now, what in the world is the matter?"

He clutched his hands in his lap and licked his lips. "Regina. Everyone's afraid to tell you, but I felt someone really had to."

"Tell me *what?*"

"Oh, Regina. I'm so sorry."

"Marcus, please. Sorry about what?"

"Oh, Regina."

"Marcus, take a few deep breaths. Good. Now say what it is you're sorry about."

He looked down at his clenched hands, then over at the television set. At last he managed to look at Regina. He said in a pained whisper, "Patrick Jones wants custody of his daughters, Regina. He doesn't love you. He married you because he needs someone to be a real mother to them. And you were perfect. I know, because I was over at the Hole in the Wall last night, and Oggie Jones was bragging about how last year Patrick swore to get his girls back. Oggie claims he told Patrick then that he'd better find himself a decent wife first, because Patrick doesn't have a clue about how to raise those girls. And so he did find himself a decent wife. You."

Regina smiled softly. "I see."

Marcus slowly shook his head. "Oh, you are so very brave and strong, to take it like this."

"Marcus, I already knew."

"Oh." He looked thoroughly nonplussed, then hastened to insist, "No, you couldn't have known..."

"Yes. Patrick has told me he wants his children back."

"Well, certainly you would say that. Be loyal to him, even after everything. You're a wonderful woman, Regina, and I..."

Marcus's voice trailed off as both he and Regina heard the sound of footsteps on the porch.

"Oh, dear," Regina murmured to herself, as the front door swung inward and she saw her husband standing on the other side of it.

On the natural stone mantel across the room, the clock struck noon. Evidently, Patrick had decided to surprise his wife and join her for lunch.

Chapter Ten

Regina *was* surprised. "Patrick! I didn't expect you."

"I can see that." He looked from the suddenly pale Marcus to his wife and back again. "What the hell is this?"

Regina swallowed and forced herself to answer. "Marcus asked to speak with me."

"About what?"

Marcus spoke up then, though his thin voice shook. "I came to tell her why you married her. I felt she should know."

Patrick's lips drew back from his teeth. "You did, huh?" Slowly he began crossing the room toward the other man. "You're one hell of a helpful guy."

Regina grew alarmed. "Patrick. Don't start anything."

Patrick grunted. "I won't. It's already started."

"Patrick!"

"I am not a violent man," Marcus quakingly explained.

Patrick took Marcus by the shirtfront. "Well, that's too damn bad for you," he said into the other man's terrified face. "Because I am."

"Patrick," Regina commanded. "Let him go. Let him go, now."

Patrick froze. Marcus, held above the ground, went on quaking. And then Patrick shoved him away. Marcus fell backward onto the couch.

"Get out," Patrick said. He turned his back and walked to the stone mantel where he remained, facing the wall.

Marcus scrambled upright and then brushed off his slacks and straightened his rumpled shirt. He combed his mussed hair with his hands.

Then he cleared his throat.

But before he could say a word, Patrick, still turned away, silkily advised, "Are you deaf? I said get the hell out of my house."

Marcus glanced nervously at Regina.

She gave him a reassuring nod. "Yes, Marcus. Please go."

Marcus, looking both relieved and reproachful, strode swiftly across the room. As he left, he quietly pulled the door closed behind him.

After Marcus was gone, Regina let the silence stretch out, because she really did dread the things she and Patrick were probably going to end up saying to each other. She wished she was a little younger and still capable of believing that a jealous display was a sign of a man's love. If she could believe that, then she could tell herself that Patrick was in love with her.

But she couldn't believe it. Patrick was a Jones, that was all. A man who didn't like anyone encroaching on what he considered his. What she'd just witnessed wasn't a lover's jealousy. It was a demonstration of ownership. Patrick had chosen her as a proper wife, one fit to raise his children. And a proper wife did not invite her old boyfriends into her home while her husband was at work.

Eventually she grew tired of standing there, waiting for him to turn around and start yelling at her. So she said briskly, "Well, I suppose you'd like lunch. I'll just go on in the kitchen and see what I can put together." She started to leave.

She got about two steps.

"Stay here." Patrick turned to face her. "What the hell was he doing here?"

"Patrick, maybe we should talk about this after you've cooled down a little."

"Answer me."

"I—"

"Answer."

"All right." She drew in a breath. "He was here for just the reason he said. He wanted me to know that you married me to get custody of Marnie and Teresa. I told him I already knew that."

"And that's all?"

"He didn't seem to believe that I knew."

"I'll bet. What else?"

"That's all."

He was silent. Then, "You said you'd keep away from him."

"I know, but he was very upset. I felt sorry for him. He wanted to talk in private, so I let him in."

Patrick seemed to be studying her, measuring what she'd told him for its veracity. Then he said, "Once, you walked away when I called to you, pretended you didn't notice when I waved. You ran off like a scared rabbit every time I looked your way for a damn week. For *his* sake. Didn't you?"

She knew he was talking about that final week before the day on Sweetbriar Summit.

"Didn't you?" It was a demand. He leaned an elbow on the mantel and waited for her to confirm what he already knew.

She gave him the truth he demanded. "Yes."

"And, knowing Marcus Shelby, I'll bet he never even had to ask you to do it. He's the type of guy who doesn't make demands on a woman. He just acts wounded until she does things his way. Am I right?"

"Patrick—"

"Answer me. Am I right?"

"Yes, you're right."

"But now, you're with *me*. And I'm a guy who does make demands. And I did ask you to stay away from him."

Though she knew she was pulling the tiger's tail, she simply could not resist pointing out, "You hardly *asked*."

He shrugged. "Fine. I didn't ask. I *told* you to stay away from him. And you said you would. But you didn't. Instead, you *invited* him into my damn house." He straightened from the mantel. "Why is that?"

"I..."

He began walking toward her. "Why?"

Her throat went dry. She had to swallow. "Because..."

"Tell me."

"Because I just...I don't *feel* anything for him. I don't know if I ever did. It was just completely *safe* to be alone with him."

"It was *safe*?" Patrick repeated, as he kept on coming.

"Yes." She backed up, but ran into the stool of her piano, which he and his brother, Brendan, had moved over from the other house three days before. She stammered on, "But, it—it was never *safe* to be alone with you. You just were...not safe. And when I realized that, I tried to stay away from you. Until the day of the picnic, when I found out it wasn't any use to try to stay away from you. Because you are a ... relentless kind of man.''

Patrick reached her and stopped. He was so close that his chest brushed her breasts. She almost dropped to the stool, but he caught her shoulders and held her erect.

"You're right," he murmured into her upturned face. "I always get what I'm after. And I am not safe. Never forget that."

She gulped. "Don't worry, I won't."

He grunted, a very self-satisfied sound. She could see that he was mollified. Probably by her admission that he was someone she'd been afraid to be alone with—while Marcus Shelby wasn't. Lately, in her state of marital bliss, it was too easy to forget what a hooligan she'd married.

She decided she had a thing or two to say to him. "Patrick, you really terrified the poor man."

"Good. Maybe he'll stay away from my wife."

"I do not approve of your behavior."

"Fine. Keep away from other men, and my behavior will improve."

She looked up at him and *almost* blurted out, *Of course I will, you fool. I have no interest in other men. Only in you. I love you. Even though you don't love me.*

But she didn't. She had some pride, after all.

She told him, "All right. I swear to you, I won't so much as go near Marcus Shelby ever again."

He grinned. "Good." And then he lowered his mouth and ran his tongue along the seam where her lips were pressed disapprovingly together.

She turned her head away. "If you think I'm going to make love with you now..."

He chuckled, a chuckle that made the muscles of her belly contract. "I do. I do think that," he confessed in a voice that was stunning in its utter guilelessness. "Come on, Gina. I came all the way home..."

"For lunch."

"Aw, Gina. Why is it always food with you?" His hands gentled on her shoulders and began a slow, deep massage.

"You should eat."

"I should get a kiss from my wife."

"Patrick..."

He lowered his mouth and grazed her chin with his teeth. "Gina..."

And then his mouth was on hers. She sighed. Her reluctance faded away while her lips parted to allow the entrance of his seeking tongue.

A few moments later, when he scooped her up against his chest and hauled her off down the hall, she thought, somewhat inchoately, that she lived in the eye of a tornado. Powerful natural forces whirled around her. And sometimes they scooped her up and carried her away.

The phone rang the next morning just as Regina and Patrick were sitting down to breakfast. Regina was the one who answered.

"Regina? It's Marybeth."

"Oh, hello. How are you?" Patrick was looking at Regina with an eyebrow raised, so she tipped the phone beneath her chin and mouthed, "Marybeth," at him.

"I'm fine," Marybeth said. "Listen, I want you to know, I was really surprised when you two called last week. But, you know, the more I thought about it, the more I realized that it's a terrific thing, you two getting together. Of course, I never really knew you. But you've always seemed to me to be a very calm and levelheaded person. You might kind of... balance Patrick out a little."

"Well..." Regina couldn't help but respond to the sincerity in the other woman's voice. "Thank you."

"Don't thank me. I mean it."

"Well, good."

"So, um, welcome to the family," Marybeth said. "Would you put Patrick on now, please?"

"Certainly," she said. "He's right here. You take care." Regina held the phone across the table and Patrick took it.

"Yeah?" he said, and then listened.

Faintly, Regina could hear the low drone of Marybeth's voice, even from across the table, though of course she couldn't make out the words. But whatever she was saying, Patrick didn't like it. As he listened, his jaw tensed. His mouth became a grim line and two creases formed between his brows.

Then he said, "You *what?*"

The faint voice on the other end of the line spoke faster.

Patrick cut in. "Yeah, I wanted them to visit, but not like this. Why didn't you *call* me? How could you put a twelve-year-old and a nine-year-old on a bus *alone* for a two-thousand-mile trip across the country?" Marybeth said something. "I don't give a damn how responsible Teresa is for her age. She's *twelve,* for crying out loud."

Marybeth began talking again. Patrick stood up and paced the floor. When he spoke, he shouted into the phone.

"Oh, right. They'll be fine, sure. But what if they're not fine? What the hell are we going to do if they don't turn up in Sacramento like they're supposed to? It's a big country out there, between Little Rock and here, just in case you didn't notice, Marybeth!"

Marybeth said something more. Regina did her best to signal Patrick to keep calm. When he refused to look her way, she got up and went to him. She took his arm. He shook her off.

"So what if you have to work? You could have called *me*. I would have come to get them, or sent the plane fare. That's the problem with you, Marybeth. You don't bother to *communicate*. You do what you want to do and when it all blows up in our faces, you say you didn't have any choice. You couldn't afford plane fare and you couldn't go with them because you had to work, as if there was nothing else in the whole damn world that you could have done. As if calling me and seeing what I was willing to do wasn't even a possibility. You're a damn disaster, Marybeth." His voice rose to a roar. "And who do you think pays for the way you mess up? Two innocent girls, that's who! Two poor, confused kids!"

From the other end of the line, Marybeth shouted right back.

"Okay, okay," Patrick growled. "So maybe I wasn't willing to do a hell of a lot for a while there. But now I am. Now Regina and I are married and I've got a nice place for the two of them to live." Regina knew what was coming. She signaled frantically for Patrick to calm down, not to make this an adversarial issue. But she was signaling in vain.

Patrick blustered on. "And that's what I want. I want them living with me! Right now, I'm the one in a good position to give them a normal life. You know you're working half the night sometimes lately, trying to get that business of yours off the ground. And they miss their family. They miss their friends. When they get here, I want them to stay here. I want them to—"

Marybeth started talking again.

"*What?*"

She said something else.

Patrick, who had stopped pacing, dropped into his chair again. "I see," he said, sounding stunned now. "All right, then. Good." Marybeth talked some more. Patrick said, "I will." Then he looked up at Regina and mouthed, "Pencil and paper."

Swiftly she found what he wanted and he wrote down the date and time that his daughters would arrive at the bus terminal in Sacramento.

Then he said, "Okay. All right. And, Marybeth. Oh, hell. I guess part of our problem was that I never gave you enough damn credit. Yeah." He was actually smiling. "You, too." He hung up.

And then he put his elbows on the table and cradled his head in his hands.

Regina couldn't stand the suspense. She blurted out, "Well? What did she say?"

Patrick lifted his head and rubbed his eyes.

"Patrick? Please, tell me."

"She said . . ."

"Yes?"

He dragged in a breath. "She's been giving it a lot of thought lately and she has to agree with me. It's all too much for her. The girls need more supervision." Patrick paused.

Regina prompted, "And?"

"The girls are on their way. And we've just agreed they will stay here through the school year."

Regina stared at him, hardly daring to believe. And then he threw back his head, opened his mouth and let out a howl of joy at the ceiling. After that, he jumped up, grabbed Regina and spun her around until she was so dizzy, she didn't know up from down.

And then he kissed her—a long, delirious kiss. Regina felt dizzier than when he'd been spinning her around. She tried to point out that their breakfast was growing cold, but then he kissed her some more.

Breakfast was forgotten. Patrick went to work late.

Chapter Eleven

"The guy sitting behind us when we left Dallas was a pervert," Marnie said.

"Hush," Teresa chided, sounding more like Nellie Anderson than a twelve-year-old.

"Hush yourself, *Saint* Teresa," Marnie replied.

They were on their way home from the bus terminal in Sacramento, where the girls had appeared on time, looking grubby and tired, but otherwise unharmed. Patrick had already told them that they would be living in North Magdalene for the coming school year. They were thrilled at the news.

And they'd been at each other's throats since the moment they got in the Bronco.

"You are impossible," Teresa hissed.

"And you're a big pain." Marnie faced the front seat and spoke to the adults. "And that guy *was* a pervert, I swear."

"He was not," Teresa firmly contended. Then she was the one addressing the front seat. "The man did look a little strange, actually. But he never bothered us." She glanced disapprovingly at her sister. "And you have no idea what a pervert is, anyway."

"Do so."

Teresa, not deigning to reply to such a childish challenge, spoke again to the grown-ups. "Honestly, I hope you can do something with her, Regina. She's impossible."

Marnie stuck the end of a yard-long licorice whip in her mouth and bit off a chunk, after which she calmly advised her older sister, in the bluntest of terms, to have sexual intercourse with herself.

Teresa gasped in outrage.

Patrick shouted over his shoulder at Marnie, "What did you say?"

Regina warned softly, "Patrick..."

But it was too late. Marnie was already repeating the advice she'd given to Teresa.

Patrick swung the wheel of the Bronco sharply to the right, causing the driver in the car behind them to blast his horn long and loudly. The Bronco bounced onto the shoulder of the road. Patrick had to do a little fancy maneuvering to get the vehicle to stop before they hit a steel-reinforced fence. The 4×4 shook and shuddered, but came to a halt just in time.

Then Patrick whirled to confront his younger daughter. "Let's get this clear right up front. Now that you're gonna be with me and Regina, you're gonna learn to control that mouth of yours."

Marnie folded her hands over her thin chest and glared at him as he glared at her. At that moment, Regina thought, the family resemblance between father and daughter was quite remarkable.

Patrick demanded, "Apologize to your sister."

Marnie pressed her lips together and went on glaring.

A stare-down ensued, Jones to Jones. Regina looked from father to daughter and concluded that little Marnie was a darn sight braver than Marcus Shelby—or probably just about any other mere man when confronted with the wrath of a Jones.

"You *will* apologize," Patrick said. "Or we'll sit here all day."

Marnie raised the nose that resembled Patrick's and looked out her side window at a tanker truck as it roared by.

Regina decided something had to be done. The first thing, she determined, was to separate the two girls so that further disturbances could be stopped before they started.

She pushed open her door. A wall of hot air hit her in the face. Though the Bronco was air-conditioned, the temperature outside was well over a hundred degrees.

Patrick barked, "What do you think you're doing, Regina?"

But she only blithely opened the door on Teresa's side of the back seat. "Teresa, would you sit in front, please?"

Teresa, who probably would have jumped off a cliff if an adult had instructed her to, obligingly got out and took Regina's seat in front.

Regina slid in next to Marnie. "Patrick," she said, "I think, if we're going to just sit here, that you ought to turn off the engine."

He shifted his glare from his daughter to his wife. Regina gave him a warm smile. His eyes narrowed. Then he shrugged. He turned in his seat and gave the key a twist.

They sat in silence while other cars rushed by them. Within ten minutes, the Bronco was an oven. They rolled down the windows.

Regina murmured, "My, it certainly is a hot day." She turned to Marnie. "We left the air-conditioning on at home, of course."

Marnie said nothing. She doggedly chewed her licorice whip down to the end.

"Luckily for all of us," Regina said, casually wiping sweat from the back of her neck, "we've got all day."

Patrick and Teresa made noises of agreement. Marnie merely looked stubborn, slightly befuddled and very hot. Unfortunately for her, the sun was slanting in at its worst from her corner of the vehicle.

Regina rested her head against the door. She sighed and closed her eyes. The heat was quite draining. It occurred to her that if she did doze off, she was likely to feel dried-out and exhausted when she woke. But Patrick had laid down an ultimatum.

Regina herself would never have made the ultimatum at this point. However, now that it *was* made, she felt that she and Patrick would lose acres of ground with his recalcitrant youngest child if they backed down. So she shifted around in the seat until she was as comfortable as she could get. The heat seemed to settle around her, broken only by the hot winds stirred up when a big rig roared past.

Regina felt herself being dragged toward a heavy, uncomfortable sleep.

And then Marnie mumbled, "Okay, okay. I'm sorry, Teresa."

Hiding her smile, Regina sat up. "Teresa?"

Teresa looked over the seat, her expression alert and agreeable. "Yes?"

"It is customary to acknowledge an apology when one is offered."

Teresa's hazel eyes shifted. Regina understood that Patrick's older daughter had hoped to avoid having to reply to her sister's grudging declaration. But of course, since she was the "good girl," she would have to say something, now that Regina had pointed out her lapse.

"All right," she nobly intoned. "I accept your apology, Marnie."

"Good," Regina said. "Now, Patrick. May we go?"

For an answer, Patrick started the engine.

The rest of the ride was very quiet. Regina thought everyone was being careful not to start anything, because they didn't know what might happen if they did. Regina felt satisfied with this.

For once, she found herself thinking of her own mother with pure fondness. Anthea Black had been a master at getting just what she wanted without ever raising her voice. Regina knew now that what she'd learned from her mother was going to come in very handy.

At home, Teresa enthused over her white wicker bedroom. "It's just beautiful, Regina. It's like something from a magazine. And it's really all mine?"

Regina nodded, "Yes, it's all yours."

Then Teresa's happy look faded.

"Teresa, what's wrong?"

"Oh, well. I get confused."

"About what?"

"Well, it's good to be grateful, isn't it?"

"Well, *I* certainly think so."

"But it's a sin to love worldly things."

"Who told you that?"

"It's in the Bible." Teresa looked more confused than ever. "I'm sure it is. Somewhere."

"Well," Regina pointed out gently, "I personally believe, along with you, that gratitude is a very good thing. And so is appreciation. And it's never wrong to be grateful for, and to appreciate, um, worldly things. As long as we never start thinking that worldly things are the most important things."

Teresa's pale brows drew together as she pondered. Then she nodded. "That makes sense."

Apparently relieved that it was okay to like her new room, Teresa hoisted her big suitcase onto the dresser and began transferring her neatly folded clothes into the empty drawers. Regina sat on the edge of the bed and watched her, thinking that Teresa was a little like she herself had been at twelve, so dutiful, she verged on obsequious. So well behaved, it made one nervous. A child who put her clothing away in drawers long before any adult had a chance to tell her to.

"All our winter things are still at Mom's," Teresa said.

Twelve years old, Regina thought, and she's worried about her winter clothing in July.

"Don't worry," Regina reassured the girl. "We'll see that everything you need gets here in time, one way or another."

Teresa looked at Regina. "I believe you. I can see that you're a very well-organized person." The words were said in a tone of mingled regard and relief. "My mom's not very well organized. She never has been. It drives me crazy, you know?" Teresa's face flushed red. She hastened to add, "Not that I don't love her a lot. I do."

Regina made a little sound of understanding, thinking that living in an orderly household would probably do a world of good for a girl like Teresa. If Teresa felt she could trust the adults around her to take care of her, she just might relax and allow herself to be a child now and then.

Right then, Teresa caught sight of her own reflection in the oval mirror over the vanity table. She was still unpacking, but she paused long enough to stand sideways and study her body's profile. "Regina, please be honest. Do you think

I'm too fat?" And then, before Regina could answer, she declared, "Not that it matters. I plan to join the Catholic church and become a nun, you know. And God loves you no matter what you look like."

Regina made no comment on Teresa's plans for the sisterhood. Instead, she softly maintained, "No, Teresa. I don't think you're too fat at all."

"Well, I don't know why I asked, anyway." Teresa carefully propped a rag doll against the pillows on the bed and put her Bible on the night table. "It's vain to worry about how you look."

Vain but natural, Regina thought, though all she did was smile in a noncommittal fashion.

Next, Regina went to see how Marnie was doing in her new room. She found the girl sitting on the floor building a space station out of one of the big plastic construction sets Patrick had put in the closet because he knew his younger daughter loved such things. Unlike Teresa's suitcase, which by then had been completely emptied and put away, Marnie's bag was still waiting untouched near the foot of the bed.

"Well, are you getting settled in all right?" Regina asked.

Marnie looked up and grunted.

"Anything I can do to help?"

"Yeah." She held up a miniature spaceman—minus a head. "Find this guy's head."

Gamely, Regina crouched on the floor and went through the box of snap-together plastic pieces. "Is this it?" She held up a head with a helmet on it.

"Yeah. Thanks." Marnie took the head and attached it to the torso and then put the little man in what appeared to be some sort of space shuttle. "Now I need four more of these." She held up a gray triangular piece.

Regina looked through the box some more and eventually found what Marnie needed. Gradually, the Alpha Galactrix Space Outpost took shape. Regina helped as Marnie allowed her to, finding pieces and sometimes even being told she could snap them in place.

As she worked alongside the child, Regina learned that Marnie thought the oak furniture in her room was "cool," and she was glad Regina hadn't "grossed her out" by giving her the same "sissy stuff" as Teresa had in her room.

"I mean, only a *girl* would want furniture made out of sticks and painted white."

Regina managed to keep from pointing out that Marnie herself was a *girl*.

Marnie was also glad that she and Teresa wouldn't have to share a room. Regina fully agreed with Marnie on that one. After seeing the way the two of them bickered and battled, Regina herself was downright *thrilled* that her new stepdaughters would not be sharing a room.

Eventually, Regina left Marnie alone and went downstairs to see about getting dinner together, the main course of which was to be chicken barbecued by Patrick. Though Regina intended that the girls would start helping with meal preparations soon enough, for that first night she and Patrick did everything.

They'd decided to eat on the back patio, which, due to an awning and the many trees in the backyard, was usually fairly cool by early evening. When all was ready, the girls were called to the table.

Marnie came first. One glance at her hands and Regina came to a decision. It was true that she wanted to be easy on Patrick's daughters for their first day in their new home. But no one was sitting down to *her* table with hands that looked as if they'd just been used to build a mud hut.

"Marnie, please go wash your hands."

Marnie shot her new stepmother a mutinous look and sprinted for the kitchen door. She was back in under thirty seconds.

"That was quick," Regina said mildly.

Marnie merely slid into her place. "Gimme the rolls."

"We will say grace before dinner," Regina announced.

Patrick made a face but said nothing.

Teresa glowed, no doubt at the prospect of living in a house where God was appreciated.

Marnie muttered something that was probably offensive, but spoken too low for anyone to be sure.

Regina gave her younger stepdaughter a tolerant smile. "But first, Marnie, before we say grace, you will go in and wash properly."

Marnie glanced sideways and then back. It was obvious she had thought this was a battle she'd won. And now here it was again. She muttered, "I did wash."

"Excuse me, I can't hear you."

"I said, I *did* wash."

"You *did* wash?"

"Yeah."

"With what?"

"Whaddaya mean, with what?"

"I mean that, whatever you used before, *now* you will go in and wash with soap and water."

"Or else what?"

Regina only smiled.

Marnie glared and groaned. She dragged herself up from the picnic table and trudged inside. A few minutes later, she returned and took her seat again, looking wounded and proud. Her hands were much cleaner than when she had left.

Regina said a brief prayer.

They began to eat. Twice, Regina reminded Marnie that, while barbecued chicken could be eaten with the fingers, it was common courtesy to wipe one's hands on one's napkin, not on one's clothing. Marnie, surprisingly, seemed to bear the criticism well enough from Regina. There were a few mumbled curses, which Regina pointedly ignored.

Both times when Marnie mumbled, Patrick looked up sharply and started to reprimand her. But Regina managed to catch his eye before he said anything. She gave him a narrowed look and a quick shake of her head so that he subsided before he got started.

But then Marnie rubbed her greasy hands on her shirt one more time.

Regina pointed out, "Please use your napkin, Marnie."

And Teresa just had to chime in, "Really, it's no use trying to teach *her* table manners. She's such a pig."

That did it. Marnie's blue eyes flashed. "Don't call me a pig, you..." She finished by using one of her favorite expletives.

Patrick's face went crimson. He stood. "Go to your room."

Marnie was outraged. "But she's always—"

"Now!"

Marnie scowled at her father for a moment. Then she leapt up and disappeared into the house.

Patrick glanced from Regina to Teresa, as if daring either of them to say a single word. Then he sat back down and picked up his fork.

After a few minutes of uncomfortable silence, the three remaining diners relaxed a little. Regina remarked on how good the chicken was. Teresa agreed, and asked for another piece.

Patrick teased, "Better watch it, Tessy, or you'll get fat as a cow."

Teresa looked up. Her face was flushed, her eyes brimmed with tears. Without a word, she stood from the table and ran into the house.

After a moment of staring with his mouth open, Patrick asked, "What did I do?"

Regina sipped from her ice tea. "Generally, Patrick, it is unwise to tease a twelve-year-old girl about her weight."

Patrick sighed. "Thank God you're here."

After the table was cleared away, Regina went to speak with Teresa, whom she found sitting in the wicker rocker, staring out the window at the catalpa tree in the backyard.

"May I come in?"

Teresa turned her head, looked at her stepmother, then looked back out the window. "If you want."

Regina closed the door behind her and sat on the edge of the bed. She looked out the window with Teresa for a while.

Teresa said, "For a whole year, all I wanted was to be home."

Regina softly pointed out, "That's what your father's wanted, too. To have you home."

"You think so?"

"I know so."

Teresa sighed. "I could hardly believe it, that someone like you would marry someone like him."

Regina chuckled. "A lot of people can hardly believe it. But it's true."

Now Teresa looked at Regina. "You . . . you really like him, don't you?"

"Mm-hmm. I really do."

Teresa shook her head and looked out the window some more. "He thinks I'm fat."

"No, he doesn't. He was teasing you. Sometimes he lacks . . . finesse."

Teresa grunted. "Does he ever. Sometimes I *hate* being a Jones. It's so unrefined. People talk about us all the time because we do crazy things. I wanted to be different than that. I thought I'd be glad to move away where no one knew what it meant that my name was Jones. But then all I wanted to do was come home."

"Life can be very confusing," Regina agreed. "Now come on." She stood and held out her hand. "We saved you a piece of strawberry shortcake."

"I can't. It's so fattening."

"Eat it without the whipped cream. Strawberries and a little sponge cake. No calories at all."

"Well, maybe just a little piece."

"Okay, then. Let's go."

Teresa allowed herself to be led to the kitchen for her shortcake, which Patrick served to her.

"Tessy, I was only teasing," he said, when he set the dessert in front of her.

Teresa sniffed. "Teasing about what?"

"About your getting fat."

"Are you saying you're sorry?"

Regina tiptoed from the room, leaving Patrick to make his apologies to his daughter without anyone else listening in.

She went to the girls' bathroom and turned on the taps in the tub. Then she went to get Marnie, who barely controlled herself from using her favorite word when she heard what her new stepmother had in store for her.

"A bath? Why a *bath?*"

"Because you need one."

"I don't need a bath."

"Yes, you do."

"I took one before we left Arkansas."

"And from now on, you'll take one every night."

"*Every night?*"

"Yes. Now let's go, or the water will run over in the tub."

Marnie folded her arms and stuck out her chin. "I will not."

Regina smiled. "Yes, Marnie, you will. You will take the bath yourself, or I will *bathe* you." Purposely, Regina stressed the word *bathe*, smiling all the while.

Marnie looked worried. "You wouldn't."

"Try me."

"I'm nine years old. I don't get *bathed*."

"You do if you won't bathe yourself."

"That's disgusting." Marnie looked at her stepmother sideways. "Are you a pervert or something?"

"Well, I certainly hope not," Regina answered guilelessly. "But perhaps, while I'm *bathing* you, you'll find out for sure."

"Oh, f—"

Regina wiggled a chiding finger at Marnie, who stopped herself from uttering the forbidden word just in time. Then she turned to Marnie's suitcase, which she intended that Marnie would unpack tomorrow before lunch. She removed a set of superhero pajamas and held them out. "Well?"

With a grumbled oath too low to get her in trouble, Marnie grabbed the pajamas. Then, her jaw set, she marched out of the room and down the hall, with Regina close on her heels. When she reached the bathroom, she slammed the door in Regina's face.

"Wash thoroughly," Regina called sweetly through the door. "I'll be checking when you're done."

No answer came back—at least not one that Regina could hear. But when Marnie emerged, she was clean behind the ears and smelled appealingly of soap and water.

"Good enough?" She stuck out her chin testily.

"Yes, that's just fine. Now, go kiss your father good-night."

"Why?"

"Because you love him."

"Yuck. Love."

"Go."

Marnie trudged into the living room, where Patrick was watching one of those live police shows. Regina didn't follow her. But after a few minutes, when Marnie didn't reappear on the way to her room, Regina peeked in on them.

Marnie had squeezed into the easy chair next to her father. Her head rested on his chest and his big arm was thrown around her small shoulders. Both of them stared at the television, rapt, as a drug bust was accomplished with a battering ram.

Smiling, Regina left them alone.

When Patrick joined Regina later in their room, Patrick's eyes were soft. He undressed her slowly, kissing her everywhere, murmuring his gratitude that she had married him and made it possible for him to have another chance with his daughters.

Regina clung to him, her heart full of the love words that her pride wouldn't let her say. He stroked her body in the way that drove her crazy with wanting him and then he kissed her at her most private place. Eager, utterly excited, Regina opened herself totally to him, as he had taught her to do.

At last, when she began to wonder if it was possible to shatter into a million pieces of pure delight, he rose above her and came down upon her. They moved, together, toward a sweet and wondrous fulfillment.

At the end, as happened too often lately, Regina had to bite her lip to keep from shamelessly crying out how much she loved him.

Later, when they lay side by side in the moonlight, she gently warned that they had a lot of work to do. Both of the girls had deep insecurities, and it would take time before they learned to trust that this new home they'd come to was a home that would last.

"We'll do what we have to do," Patrick murmured sleepily. "And eventually they'll see that it'll last."

Regina cuddled close against him and tried to believe he was right.

But still, she couldn't help but wonder about the other women who must once have loved Patrick as she did now. About Chloe, who'd gone off who knew where with a stranger. And Marybeth, trying her best to make a go of it on her own, two thousand miles away.

Had Patrick once reassured them that what they shared would last?

If he had, then he'd been wrong. Regina silently prayed that he was right this time. And not only for her own selfish sake, but for the sake of two innocent children who deserved a stable home and parents they could count on.

Chapter Twelve

As Regina had suspected might happen, the ensuing few weeks were not easy ones.

Marnie fought her bath most nights and had to be constantly reminded that one ate with one's fork, not one's hands. And like her father, when she became angry, she lashed out. She'd use her fists—or that certain forbidden word—without compunction. And then she'd end up consigned to her room.

Poor Teresa, on the other hand, was so determined to be perfect that Regina often felt she was dealing with an automaton. Patrick's older daughter often seemed incapable of a spontaneous thought, a girl who was much too old for her own good. And she was incredibly sensitive to criticism. A thoughtless word, especially from Patrick who was not known for his tact, would have her scurrying away in tears.

Several times, Marybeth was brought into the battles via the telephone. One or the other of the girls would call her mother in Arkansas and complain tearfully about how awful things were. The first few times that happened, Marybeth became as upset as the child who had called her. But then, Regina convinced Patrick that he should talk to Marybeth about the problem. He called Marybeth. Together, they agreed on how they would handle such incidents from then on.

After that, when one of the girls called her mother to complain, Marybeth would listen sympathetically and then say, "Well, you know you can always return here to live with me. But your father and I have agreed on one thing. There'll be no bouncing back and forth. If you come back here to live, then here's where you'll stay." Since neither of the girls really wanted to leave North Magdalene, that would settle them down, at least temporarily.

But peaceful moments were few and far between. And whenever things did settle down, then Marnie would say something and Teresa would reprimand her and the two of them would be off and bickering.

The house echoed with slamming doors, with Marnie's curses and Teresa's sobs. As July faded into August, Patrick's dream of having his girls home was, more often than not, a nightmare.

Through it all, Regina was the peacemaker. And she was grateful that the girls seemed to accept her. Though it often took every last ounce of patience Regina possessed, she was scrupulously careful to be calm, consistent, kind and firm with them. The girls, neither of whom had any idea how to manipulate a person who refused to be intimidated or to lose her temper, soon concluded that their new stepmother could not be maneuvered.

Though Regina found their lives a constant strain, she learned much. And every day she grew to care more deeply for Marnie, who was so cocky, bold and bright. And for the gentler, sadder Teresa, whose smile was just like her father's and who longed to be small-boned and delicate—and longed to dedicate herself to good works.

All told, Regina was happy the girls had moved in. But their constant presence in the house ended the extended honeymoon she and Patrick had enjoyed before their arrival.

Since his daughters were in and out all day, Patrick no longer came home from work during his lunch break to carry his new bride off to the bedroom and make love to her until she begged him never to stop. And with all the problems they were having as a family, sometimes days would go by without his turning to Regina in the night.

Regina knew that their less frequent lovemaking was natural, given the stresses they were suffering. She refused to think that her new husband might already be tiring of her as a lover.

She did her best to keep her thoughts positive. Though they made love less often, Patrick did begin to tell her things about himself and his past that he'd never opened up about before. She saw that as a very good sign.

One night, after a particularly unpleasant battle with Marnie, when the poor child had been sent to bed straight from the dinner table for the second evening in a row, Regina helped Teresa finish the dishes. Then Regina went out to the service porch and folded the last load of laundry. Finally, she wandered upstairs to the master bedroom where she found Patrick sitting on the edge of the bed wearing only a pair of gym shorts and staring at his bare feet.

Quietly she closed the door, set the folded clothes she was carrying on the dresser by the walk-in closet and went to sit opposite him in the rocking chair by the window. He gave her a quick, cheerless smile and then resumed regarding his toes.

She got up from the rocker and went to sit next to him on the bed. "What's the matter?" she asked gently when he volunteered nothing.

He shook his head. She smoothed his hair back, where it had fallen over his forehead. It was still wet from the shower he'd just taken.

"Come on." She gave him a gentle nudge with the side of her body. "Get it out. You'll feel better if you do."

"Aw, Gina."

"Yes?"

He swore.

"Keep going."

He chuckled, a humorless sound. Then he fell back on the bed and laced his hands on his bare chest.

"Talk," she urged again.

"Oh, all right." He gave a deep sigh. "I knew I was a lousy father. I swear I did. I just didn't know how lousy. Till lately."

"Oh, Patrick..."

He glanced at her, his expression wry. "Come on, Gina. Don't let me talk that way about myself. Think of something nice to say, like how I'm not *that* bad."

She couldn't suppress a smile. "Okay. You're not *that* bad."

He grunted. "Not very convincing. And maybe it's better to tell the truth, anyway. I started out lousy, and I've pretty much stayed that way."

"What do you mean, you started out lousy?"

He stared up at the slowly rotating ceiling fan, another of the myriad of improvements made by the two ladies from Oakland from whom Patrick had bought the house. Regina waited as he seemed to study the fan. But after a while, when he didn't say anything, she began to think he wouldn't answer her.

She was mildly surprised when he finally spoke. "I married Marybeth because she was pregnant with Teresa. Did you know that?"

She tried to be tactful. "There was a rumor to that effect around town."

He grunted. "That stands to reason. There's always a rumor around this town." He watched the fan some more.

Regina took the moment to toe off her shoes and stretch out beside him.

He turned to give her a sad smile. Then he looked at the ceiling again and confessed softly, "The problem was, when I married Marybeth, I was still in love with Chloe."

Regina tried not to stiffen when she heard that. She wanted to know what was in her husband's mind and heart, to understand what his life had been like in all the years before he had made her his wife. She didn't want to be judgmental. But she couldn't help feeling dismayed that he would have made love to one woman while he was *in* love with another.

Patrick went on, still watching the fan, "Okay, I've lied to myself and everyone else for years, trying to pretend there was never much between Chloe and me. I don't know why I bothered with the lie. No one ever believed it. It eased my pride, I guess, since she took my heart in her pretty little hands and broke it right in two."

Regina lay very still. Right then, hearing him say such things about another woman, she understood exactly what Patrick meant when he spoke of his broken heart—and his pride.

Lately, since their lives had grown more complicated, it grew harder every day to live with the fact that he didn't return her love. Sometimes it seemed her pride was the only thing that kept her heart in one piece. As long as he didn't know she was in love with him, they were equals. She'd wanted a husband and family. He'd needed a wife. They were a match in what they brought to each other.

But if he knew of her hopeless, hungry love for him, the scales of their relationship would be dangerously tipped. Instead of an equal, she'd be the needy one. The one who yearned for something he was never going to give.

Patrick was watching her. "What's wrong?"

"Nothing," she lied. "Go on."

"You sure?"

"Yes. Please. Continue."

He turned his head away and rubbed his face with his hand. "Hell. Anyway, when Teresa was born, I was too wrapped up in my own damn broken heart to pay much attention to her. And I was a bad husband to Marybeth, I know that. I never gave her the care and affection she deserved as my wife." He looked at Regina again. "Hey."

"What?" She forced a smile.

"Look. It wasn't like you're thinking."

"How do you know what I'm thinking?"

"I can see it in your eyes. You think I got Marybeth pregnant when I was still with Chloe. But I wasn't *with* Chloe. Chloe had broken up with me for the hundredth time, for some reason I can't even remember now. Chloe was...I don't know. It was like she didn't want me when she could have me. But then, the minute I was unavailable, I was the only man for her. I got fed up with it, that was all, even though I was still really gone on her. Finally, she told me she was through with me one time too many. I decided it didn't matter if I could never get over her, I'd damn well live without her."

He turned to his side, facing Regina, and braced himself on an elbow. "Then, I was out one night and I met Marybeth. She seemed so open and friendly." Idly, he stroked Regina's pinned-up hair, finding a loose curl that he began rolling around his finger. "She didn't play all the games Chloe always seemed to play."

Regina remembered what he'd said, the morning after their marriage, about the *rotten games* that men and women could play. She felt it was time to ask, "What games?"

"Ah, Gina." He sighed, a tired kind of sigh. "How can I explain it to someone like you?"

"Like me?"

"Yeah. You don't play games. You say *yes* or you say *no* and what you say is what you mean. But with Chloe, at least when it came to me, *yes* might mean *maybe* or *no* or *check with me tomorrow* or any number of damn things. To be with a woman like that can be exciting—for a while, anyway. It's a fake kind of high, to battle it out with a woman like that. You never know what will happen next.

"But you can't...build anything that lasts with a woman like that. And I knew that in my head before the rest of me caught on. So I finally swore to myself I was through with her. And I met Marybeth and we started going together, Marybeth and me, even though I was still carrying a torch for Chloe. And then it turned out Marybeth was pregnant. So we got married. And the marriage never really seemed to work out. But Marybeth was determined to keep trying. And I... Hell, I felt guilty all the time, because I still had this thing for Chloe."

Regina decided she'd always wonder, if she didn't ask, "Did you...cheat on Marybeth, with Chloe?"

Patrick dropped the strand of hair he'd been toying with. Regina had never seen him look so hurt. "Never. Damn it,

Regina. I *am* a Jones, after all. We drive our women crazy, but we *never* cheat on them.''

Regina realized she believed him. The relief she felt was a lovely thing. It came to her then that she couldn't bear it if he were to cheat on her. Though he didn't return her love, at least he was a loyal spouse.

''Anyway—'' he stretched out on his back again ''—Marybeth and I never had much of a marriage. But gradually, I did get over Chloe. And then I started thinking that maybe Marybeth and I could make it work after all. So there was a year or so there where we were both trying our damnedest to have a real marriage together. That was when Marnie came along.'' Patrick groaned and rubbed his eyes with his fingers. The gesture spoke eloquently of his bottomless weariness with himself and his own crazy past.

Regina ached for him, for his confusion and for the sadness of the story he'd just told. She thought of everyone involved. Of Patrick. Chloe. Marybeth. Somehow, not one of them had managed to get what they wanted.

''They say that Marybeth divorced *you*,'' Regina murmured. ''Is that true?''

''Yeah. She told me she finally realized she wasn't going to get the kind of love she wanted from me. So she decided to cut her losses and give it up. And though it was tough on the girls, I guess it wasn't any tougher than having their parents either at each other's throats or not speaking to each other all the time, trying to keep a bad marriage together.

''And in general, since the divorce, Marybeth and I have gotten along much better than we ever did while we were married. Marybeth's a good woman, really. I like her. But we never really worked well together. She would cry and be wounded about every little thing. And then I would get mad and storm out. We just couldn't get it together, you know?''

''I think so.''

He propped himself on his elbow again and ran a finger slowly down her arm. "I think it takes a very levelheaded woman to make a life with me."

She warmed at the oblique compliment. "Oh, does it?"

"You bet."

Regina knew she shouldn't ask the next question, but somehow it was on her lips anyway. "Patrick, um, it's better if I know the truth. I know you said you're over Chloe. But, deep in your heart, are you sure that's the truth?"

He was looking at her. His face was very still, completely unreadable. "Yes."

Hesitantly, she dared to point out, "People say you were...upset, when she left town last year."

"So?"

"Well, I mean, if you were over her..."

"Look. A lot was happening then. It just seemed like the whole world was turned upside down. Everything was changing. And I was the damn idiot standing there wondering why the hell it all seemed to be passing me by. Marybeth moved away with my kids. My sister got together with Sam Fletcher. That really threw me, you know, Delilah and Sam together, after all those years when they hated each other. My old man almost gave the Mercantile building to Sam to get him to marry Delilah. See, my dad was desperate to get my sister a husband. Did you know that?"

"I think I heard that story, yes."

"Well, the Mercantile had always been promised to me and suddenly, my dad was just going to hand it over to Sam. And at the same time Chloe started dating that guy that she eventually lit out with."

"But if you were really over her, then it shouldn't have mattered who she dated."

"Aw, Gina. You are so right. It shouldn't have mattered. And it didn't matter, except that it was one more thing that wasn't as it used to be. And also, I was a little worried about her, because I did love her once and I thought she was wrecking her life, to run off with some stranger."

Regina prompted, "And what else?"

"Hell, you are merciless."

"Come on. What else?"

"Oh, all right. It was real small-minded of me, I know, but I guess I was kind of used to the idea that even though a long time ago, Chloe broke my heart, she was still sweet on me, still pining after me. And then, suddenly, she was through pining after me. Zap. Hit me right in my foolish pride once again." He let out a rueful chuckle.

Regina allowed herself to chuckle along with him. What he said did make sense. And she felt immeasurably better, to think that maybe whatever had been between him and Chloe was truly over and done.

He lay flat again and playfully tugged on her arm. "Come here."

Obliging, she stretched out on top of him, but low enough that she could rest her chin on his chest.

"The real losers in all of this were the girls." His words made a deep, pleasant rumble against her breasts. "I know that. And I hope—" he laid his hand against her cheek "—with your help, that I can finally make it up to them."

"Oh, Patrick."

His finger brushed her lips. "What?"

"We'll work it out."

"Damn right we will." His voice was husky. With a finger, he traced each of her brows in turn.

"But you could..." She hesitated. She didn't want to criticize him, but now seemed the perfect time to delicately point out a few things.

"I could what?"

She plunged in. "Well, you could tease them less, and listen to them more. You could be affectionate instead of gruff. And you could also hold off on the ultimatums until you've thought through what those ultimatums are going to cost you—and the rest of us, for that matter."

"Hmm," he said, his fingers slipping behind her head to begin removing the pins from her hair. "Anything else I should work on?"

"That'll do for a start."

He pulled out the pins and tossed them up in the air, over the side of the bed. He was grinning.

"Patrick, stop that. Who do you think will have to pick those up?"

"Relax. I'll do it. Later."

"Of course, you say that now, but—"

"Don't get prissy."

She couldn't hide her smile. Wonderful things usually happened shortly after he called her "prissy." "I can't help it. I'm prissy." She slid her arms up his warm, hard chest and took his face in her hands. "So I guess you'll have to—"

"Make you hot." He chuckled, then grew more serious. "I don't kiss you enough anymore." He looked almost sad.

Regina wondered, as she had too often the past weeks, if he was having second thoughts about the life they now shared. She pushed the idea away and suggested shyly, "You could kiss me now."

He didn't hesitate, but took her shoulders and urged her closer. She scooted up his body and sighed as she put her lips on his.

Suddenly, with his chest against her breasts and his mouth beneath hers, her doubts and fears seemed insignificant. Though her husband did not love her and her marriage had its rough spots, she would rather be with Patrick than with all the nice, safe men the world had to offer.

And after that night, things started to improve.

Patrick seemed to take her advice to heart, because his temper stayed under control most of the time. He was more careful of Teresa's tender sensibilities. He was not so quick to banish Marnie to her room when she succumbed to her fondness for inappropriate language. There were still shouted orders, slamming doors and anguished sobs, but they didn't happen quite so often.

That weekend, Patrick borrowed his uncle Robbie Riley's boat and they went to Bullfinch Bar Reservoir as a family. They swam from the boat and took turns waterskiing and they all came home tired and happy and sunburned. Unfortunately, Marnie and Teresa ended up in a shouting match at the dinner table and they were both sent off to their rooms without dessert. But nothing was perfect, Regina decided, as she slathered aloe vera gel on her lobster-red arms.

Over the next few days, things got better still. They made it through two entire dinnertimes without anyone bursting into tears or being sent to her room.

Regina began asking for Teresa's help with some of her community activities. Teresa glowed at the idea that she was someone her stepmother would trust with such important responsibilities.

Marnie, who'd reestablished her old friendship with one of the Riggins boys, was encouraged to have the boy over whenever she wanted. So instead of disappearing into the woods right after breakfast and being impossible to locate all day, now Marnie and little Kenny spent half the time barreling around the house, or building a fort out back in the catalpa tree. There was a lot of shouting and screeching that went on, but Regina didn't mind. It was good to have Marnie near and know she was all right.

On Thursday, Regina decided to bake a cake. Both girls expressed their willingness to help, though neither had ever baked a cake before. Regina determined the two children would bake their first cake together, as an exercise in cooperation, something both of them could use a little practice in when it came to each other.

The cake turned out lopsided and the frosting was too runny. But when they brought it to the table that night, Patrick told them it was the best cake he'd ever tasted. The pride and pleasure on the two young faces had Regina turning away to hide the sentimental moisture in her eyes.

It was so clear, just looking at them. The girls had really begun to believe that their new home with their father and stepmother was a home they could put their trust in.

And then, on the second Friday in August, Chloe Swan returned to town.

Chapter Thirteen

Nellie, of course, was the one who brought the news.

Regina knew right away that something was up, because the first thing Nellie asked as Regina led her into the kitchen was, "Where are the children?"

Regina, who'd just finished cleaning up after their lunch, wiped her hands on a towel. "Teresa's gone back to Mrs. Leslie's to finish her vacuuming for her."

Nellie chose a chair and sat. "Such a sweet girl, that dear Teresa."

"And Marnie took off for Kenny Riggins's house. They're going swimming."

"So both of them are gone?" Nellie helped herself to a cluster of seedless grapes from the fruit bowl in the center of the breakfast table.

"Yes, they're both gone."

"Good."

"Why?"

Nellie pulled a grape off the stem and popped it in her mouth. "Oh, Regina. This is so difficult. I hardly know where to begin." Nellie's eyes were shining.

Regina said nothing. It didn't matter what she said, anyway. Nellie would tell it all in her own good time.

Nellie looked up at her. "Dear. I really think it's best if you sit down."

Regina repressed a tart remark and took the chair across from the older woman. "Okay, I'm sitting. And I'm listening. What is it, Nellie?"

Nellie's sigh was very long and very meaningful. "I've just come from the post office, and who do you imagine I saw there?" The question was rhetorical. Nellie finished triumphantly, "Chloe Swan."

Regina schooled her face into placid lines. "Oh, really?"

"Yes. And she looked absolutely beautiful. A little pale, perhaps. A little ... distressed. But lovely, as always, nonetheless."

"Yes, well, Chloe is a beautiful woman."

"Yes, she certainly is. She arrived back in town this morning. And she is back to stay."

"She told you this?"

"No, I spoke with her mother." Nellie had always regarded Melanie Swan, the postmistress, as a close friend. "I went in to get my mail and Chloe was there talking with her mother. And then Chloe left and it was time for Melanie's break. We went for lunch together. And Melanie told me *everything*."

"What, exactly, is *everything*, Nellie."

Nellie finished the grapes and set the picked-clean stem on the table. She leaned toward Regina and expounded in a stage whisper, "Chloe has realized that she can't go on without Patrick. So she said goodbye to that man she ran off with and returned home. She is positively *distraught* to learn that Patrick has remarried. And she plans to fight, to get him back."

"I see."

"Oh, my dear. I am so sorry."

"Sorry for what, Nellie?"

"For what is going to happen now. But I warned you, didn't I? You can never say that I didn't warn you."

"Frankly, Nellie, I think you're overreacting to this."

"Well, certainly you want to think that. And I don't blame you. Just remember, I'm here for you. When you need to talk it all out."

"How could I forget?"

Nellie sat up a little straighter. "Do I detect a note of hostility in your tone, dear?"

"Why, Nellie. What could have given you an idea like that?"

Nellie shook her head. "Oh, my dear. I know how this must be for you."

"No, you don't."

"Yes, I do. And I also realize that it's always a temptation to shoot the messenger in a situation like this."

To Regina, right then, that idea held great appeal.

"But it's all right," Nellie sniffed. "I understand. I really do. And, as always, I forgive you." With great dignity, Nellie stood. "And I know you want to be alone. So I will be going."

Regina knew very well that Nellie's true reason for leaving was so she could get home and start calling everyone with this latest bit of gossip. But Regina didn't point it out. She wasn't about to say or do anything that would keep Nellie around for one minute more than the woman had already stayed. Regina pushed back her chair and saw Nellie to the door.

Nellie patted Regina's arm just before she left. "You just call me the minute anything happens. Oh, and I almost forgot." Nellie felt in a pocket of her dress and pulled out a folded sheet of paper. "The hymns. For Sunday."

Regina took the paper and put it in her own pocket. "Thanks for dropping by." She smiled and stepped back, holding the door wide. Nellie went through it.

Swiftly Regina shut the door. She didn't even breathe until she heard the tapping of Nellie's shoes as she went down the porch steps.

Then, her hand still on the knob, she shook her head. No, she would *not* let Nellie's pettiness upset her. She would not allow her own foolish doubts to take control. She would not dwell on the thought that Chloe Swan was the one woman her husband had ever admitted to loving. And she would not obsess about how worried she'd been recently that he'd grown tired of his new wife and of their humdrum, stress-ridden life.

No matter what absurd tales Nellie insisted on passing around, it was silly to worry about Chloe Swan. Patrick could have made up with Chloe after Marybeth divorced him if he'd wanted to. And he himself had explained to Regina less than two weeks ago that his love for Chloe was firmly in the past.

And more than anything, Patrick wanted to keep custody of the girls, which was primarily contingent on his being married to a responsible woman who would create a caring home. There was no reason he'd put that in jeopardy for the sake of a love that he himself had said was long dead.

No reason except that he doesn't love me, and that he misses the old, exciting life he used to have before he settled down, Regina's worried mind whispered.

But her good sense was having none of that. She drew her shoulders up and decided to quit manufacturing problems for herself. Life was challenge enough as it was.

To soothe herself, she took the list of songs from her pocket and sat at the piano to go over them. Within fifteen minutes, the beauty of the music had worked its special magic on her heart. She felt better. And as evening approached and Teresa returned from Mrs. Leslie's, she felt better still.

Teresa came in the kitchen, snitched one of the carrots Regina was peeling and began munching on it. Regina smiled to herself. Tessy was feeling more at ease lately. It showed in a thousand little ways, like her presuming to steal a carrot that her stepmother was cutting up for their dinner.

"Guess what Mrs. Leslie told me?"

Dread tightened Regina's stomach, as all the doubts and fears she'd worked all afternoon to banish crowded back in on her once more. Was she going to hear about Chloe's return from her stepdaughter, too?

But then she relaxed. Teresa was very sensitive. It was doubtful she'd be so offhand if her news concerned the return to town of her father's old flame.

"What?" Regina asked brightly.

Teresa hesitated. She seemed to be seeking the right words. Regina's anxiety returned. Then Teresa blurted, "You used to go out with Mr. Shelby from the grocery store, right?"

Warily, Regina answered. "Yes. Why?"

"But you dropped him for Dad, didn't you?"

Regina chose another carrot and began stroking it with the peeler. "It wasn't quite that simple. But yes, right after I broke up with Mr. Shelby, your father and I were married."

"Well, what I mean is, you don't still *love* him or anything, do you? I mean, you love Dad, because he's your husband, right?"

"Um, right."

"Whew. That's good." Teresa popped the rest of the carrot in her mouth and chomped contentedly.

"Why?"

"Because last night Mr. Shelby took Angie Leslie to dinner in Nevada City."

Regina stopped peeling. She turned to her stepdaughter, who was grinning. Slowly Regina grinned back. "No."

"Yes." Teresa laughed. It was a happy, bubbling, laugh. A girl's laugh, with just a hint of the woman she would soon become. Regina had a feeling that she would hear little more about Teresa's plans to be a nun. Teresa chattered on, "Old Mrs. Leslie is just all excited about it. I mean, you know, Angie Leslie's been married about a hundred times."

"Three times," Regina corrected, trying to sound stern.

"Right. Three times. And it never worked out. And now old Mrs. Leslie thinks her granddaughter has finally found a nice, steady guy who will marry her and *stay* married to her for the rest of their lives."

Regina, who was enjoying Teresa's carefree laughter and the happy light in her eyes, had to bite her tongue to keep from saying too much. Silently, she wished Angie luck with the nonmarrying Marcus.

And who could say? Maybe Angie would be the one to make Marcus Shelby change his mind about matrimony. And then again, perhaps Angie had already experienced enough connubial bliss to last a lifetime and she and Marcus would be happy with—how had Marcus put it?—*an important and meaningful relationship, where they both had their independence and their privacy.*

Who could say? Regina shook her head.

Right then, Marnie came bouncing in smelling of river water and carrying a mason jar.

"Hey, you guys. Look. You gotta look at this." Marnie held up the jar and pointed. Regina and Teresa both bent over to peer into the jar, wherein they spotted a tadpole that was well on its way to becoming a frog. "It's got all its feet. And the head is starting to take the right shape. Pretty nifty, huh?"

"Yes," Regina agreed. "Very nifty. And surprising for so late in the year. Usually the tadpoles are all turned to frogs by now."

For a moment, even Teresa deigned to stare with interest at the almost-frog. But then she couldn't resist sniffing. "P.U. Where have you been?"

Marnie was instantly truculent. "Swimming. So what?"

"You *smell* like you've been rolling around in a pile of dead fish."

Marnie stuck out her chin. "Well, you *are* a pile of dead fish."

Teresa flipped her pale hair back over her shoulder. "Honestly. How rude. You are the most—"

Regina managed to capture Teresa's eye and give her a slight negative shake of the head. She'd had a few talks with Teresa lately about starting fights with her sister by criticizing the younger girl. Teresa had agreed to work on controlling her urge to bait Marnie under the guise of playing big sister.

"Oh, all right," Teresa grumbled, in answer to Regina's chiding look. "I'm stopping, I'm stopping." She turned and flounced from the room.

With a satisfied smirk on her face, Marnie watched Teresa's retreating back. Then she turned to Regina and held up the jar. "Can I keep him, huh, please?"

"Yes, but you mustn't put the jar in the sun, or you'll end up with a boiled frog."

"Ugh, yuck. I won't. I promise."

"And maybe tonight, after dinner, we'll go over to the other house and look for my old aquarium. It's up in the attic somewhere, I think. We could fix it up so that when your tadpole really becomes a frog, he'll have some dry land to hop on as well as water to swim in."

"Hey, yeah, Gina. You promise? We can go find the aquarium tonight?"

"Sure. Right after your bath."

Marnie made a hideous face, then burst into a huge smile. "You're tricky, Gina. You know that?"

"I have to be, around this house."

Right then, the phone rang. Regina, who was standing closest to it, picked it up. "Hello?"

There was a silence on the other end, then a click. The dial tone droned in Regina's ear. She put the phone back on the hook.

"Who was it?" Marnie wanted to know.

Regina shrugged. "Wrong number, I guess."

"Listen." Marnie was full of plans for her frog-to-be. "I think I'll go out in the backyard and look for a few good rocks." And she was out the door.

Regina watched through the window over the sink as Marnie carefully set the jar in the shade of the catalpa tree. Then she walked around the perimeter of the lawn, picking up rocks from the drain cobble Patrick had used as a border near the fence. Marnie would study each rock very carefully, and then toss it aside, or carry it over and set it in a neat little pile by the mason jar where her almost-frog was temporarily contained.

"What's going on in here?" Patrick came up behind Regina and nuzzled her neck.

"Nothing much. Fixing dinner." Regina smiled and leaned back against him. "I didn't hear you come in."

"I'm a sneaky SOB."

"How delightfully put."

"Don't get—"

"Prissy. I know."

He rubbed his chin against her hair. "What's Marnie up to out there?"

"Planning a frog condo."

"Huh?"

"You'll see, when it's done."

"Hell, with all the stuff that goes on around here, lately, I can't keep up." He stepped to the side, swiveled the faucet into the right half of the sink, and got out the special washing compound that even worked on automotive grease. "What's for dinner?" He worked the dirt and oil from his hands.

"Steaks. As soon as you barbecue them." She put the carrots on the stove and began assembling the ingredients for a tossed salad.

Patrick took the steaks from the refrigerator and sprinkled them with seasoning salt. Regina paused in washing lettuce leaves to watch him.

Her breath caught, as it so often did when she stopped to look at the man she'd married. She recalled that first day she'd really seen him. When he'd emerged from the back of a truck with his shirt off and maneuvered the refrigerator she now considered hers into the house they now shared. That day he'd seemed like someone larger, more beautiful, more passionate, more *everything* than the mere mortals who inhabited the mundane world she knew. He'd had nothing whatever to do with her and her serene, undistinguished little life.

And today he was her husband. How would she bear it if she were to lose him?

"Okay." His eyes were watchful. "What is it?"

She felt slightly abashed. "It's nothing, really."

"It's something. What?"

She blurted it out. "Chloe Swan's back in town."

He gave a noncommittal shrug. "Yeah. I know."

"How?"

"She came in. For gas."

"I see."

Now he looked a little angry. "What the hell's the matter? She came in. She asked for a fill-up. She got what she asked for. And she left."

That's all? she longed to ask. But she didn't. It would only be her own pitiful jealous heart asking a question like that. Patrick had sworn to be true to her. And she believed he had been true to her. He'd been honest and open about his past and about Chloe Swan. If she started grilling him with questions now, it would be tantamount to declaring she didn't trust him.

His expression softened. "Look, Gina. She's got nothing to do with us. Do you hear what I'm saying?"

She forced a smile. "Yes. And you're right."

"That old bat Nellie, brought you the news, right?"

Regina nodded.

"Someday somebody will silence that woman for good. It won't be pretty. I swear to you."

"Nellie has her good points."

"Name them."

"Um . . ."

"Right. Keep thinking. You'll come up with something in a year or two." He picked up the steaks and went out to fire up the barbecue.

* * *

Later, after the girls had gone to bed, Patrick and Regina rocked together for a while on the swing he'd transferred from her house. He put his arm around her and she leaned her head on his shoulder.

Since they were idly discussing the day just past, she told him what Teresa had told her about Angie Leslie and Marcus. They laughed together at the idea of the shy grocery store owner and North Magdalene's most glamorous divorcée finding happiness with each other. Hearing the laughter in his voice and feeling the warmth of his strong arm around her, Regina was absolutely certain that her distress about Chloe Swan was totally uncalled for. She resolved not to worry about the other woman anymore.

They sat, swinging and whispering together, for a while more. Then, holding hands, they went inside.

Not much later, just as Patrick was finishing up his shower and Regina was cleaning her face, the phone rang. Regina fumbled for the hand towel and went to grab the extension by the bed.

"Hello?" Once again, there was a heavy silence, after which the line was disconnected.

"Who was that?" Patrick stood in the doorway to their bathroom, wearing nothing but a questioning look and drying his hair with one of the giant bath sheets he favored.

"I don't know. Wrong number, I guess."

He shrugged and went back to the bathroom to brush his teeth.

The next day, Regina went over to Main Street in the early afternoon to pick up a few things at Marcus's store and to collect the mail.

At the store, as she stood over the open meat case and tried to decide between ground beef and pork chops, she heard singing. It was coming from the little butcher's room on the other side of the meat counter, where the meat that was stored in the locker farther back was cut up into salable portions.

She recognized the voice immediately. It was Marcus, though she'd never in her life heard him sing except when it was expected of him, at church. He was singing the Bob Dylan song "Lay, Lady, Lay," that had been popular years and years ago.

When he got to the part where he implored the lady not to wait any longer for the night to begin, Regina knew she was in trouble. If she didn't get away, she'd burst into hopeless giggles. Marcus would discover her and she would mortify the poor man.

She grabbed up both the pork chops *and* the ground beef and fled for the produce section. But the memory of Marcus's thin voice warbling out his unbridled sexual longing had her smiling all the way to the post office.

After the August heat outside, Regina found it pleasantly cool in the post office. She set her groceries on the little sorting table against the far wall and moved to the boxes, where she spun the combination dial. She had the box open and the mail in her hand when, from the corner of her eye, she saw someone emerge from the door that led to the counter area where Melanie Swan held sway.

Regina looked up, a rote smile of greeting on her face. In North Magdalene, one said hello to everyone.

Even the woman one's husband used to love, she thought grimly, as she realized she was looking into the green eyes of Chloe Swan.

"Hello, Chloe, how are you?"

She waited for Chloe's superficial, polite response.

But the response didn't come. Instead, Chloe let go of the door she'd just passed through and brought a perfectly manicured hand up to touch her own throat. Regina stared at that slim hand, at the long pink-tipped nails.

And then Chloe dropped her hand. She threw back her shoulders and raised her head high. She marched right up to Regina, her eyes like emerald flames in the lovely oval of her face.

Regina, bewildered, felt the strangest urge to bolt around the other woman and run for the open street. But she held her ground.

"Chloe? Are you all right?"

Chloe's gaze swept Regina from head to toe and back again.

"Chloe?"

And then, without a word, the woman whirled away and strode to the main door. She had shoved the door open and disappeared from sight before Regina realized she was holding her breath.

That evening, Patrick came home with a video, a comedy he'd rented from Santino's Barber, Beauty and Variety Store. Once dinner had been finished and the dishes were cleaned up, Regina made a huge bowl of popcorn. Then the girls stretched out on the floor side by side with the big bowl between them. They munched away contentedly, staring at the TV screen and dissolving into fits of giggles every five minutes or so.

Regina tried to concentrate on the movie, but her mind kept wandering. She was trying not to think about her bizarre encounter with Chloe Swan. Her success was minimal.

Halfway through the movie, the phone rang. Regina, the least absorbed of the four of them in what was happening on the screen, decided she might as well be the one to answer. She eased out of the circle of Patrick's arm and went to the phone on the low table by the piano.

When she picked up the receiver and said hello, the same thing happened as had twice the day before. There was silence, a click and then the dial tone droned in her ear.

Regina hung up. She stood by the phone table for a moment, wondering what she really didn't want to wonder: Was this some type of harassment technique of Chloe Swan's?

She sighed and shrugged. Well, at least one thing was settled. This last hang-up call was one strange thing too many. She would discuss her anxieties about Chloe as soon as she and Patrick were alone.

She went back to him at the couch. He looked up at her and smiled and her heart did a silly little flip-flop in her chest.

"Anything important?" he asked with a lift of a brow.

She shook her head and sat next to him once more. She could wait until the children were in bed to tell him that she feared his old girlfriend had set out to make her life miserable.

When she told him, Patrick was sympathetic, but not terribly concerned.

"Look. Chloe's always been a confused woman. People like her, because she can be so sweet and friendly. But then she'll really torment any poor sucker who has the bad sense to fall for her. And she does things without thinking. Like I told you before, I really was worried for her when she left town with that guy a year ago. I thought she was crazy to take off with a stranger like that. I was afraid she'd end up in big trouble. But now she's back and there's nothing wrong with her that taking a little responsibility for her life wouldn't fix. Whatever she's up to, she'll give it up if she doesn't get any response."

"Patrick, you didn't see the look in her eyes today. It was menacing. I was actually a little frightened of her. And Nellie told me that Chloe's mother said Chloe came back to town specifically to get you away from me."

Patrick swore low and feelingly. "Damn Nellie. Damn her to hell."

"Patrick, don't ..." Regina spoke softly.

Patrick pulled her close then, and stroked her hair. "I'm sorry that you have to put up with this garbage. But I swear to you, Gina, it'll pass. I'm positive." He held her face up so that he could look in her eyes. "And you can't be sure the hang-up calls aren't just a coincidence, can you?"

She shook her head, realizing she felt better just having told him. "You're right," she said. "It'll probably all blow over. It's just ... I don't know. The way she looked at me."

"Forget her," Patrick urged.

Regina agreed that she would.

But over the next two days, there were more hang-up calls. And then on Tuesday morning, while Patrick was in the bedroom getting dressed and Regina was frying bacon in the kitchen, the phone rang again. Regina picked it up a few seconds after it stopped ringing, not realizing Patrick had already answered the line in the bedroom.

Regina heard Chloe's breathless voice. "Patrick, I won't wait any longer. I must see you. Today."

Regina stifled a gasp. All conscious thought fled. Her decorous upbringing took over. The call was not for her, so she hung up, very quietly.

Then she turned back to the stove and attended to the bacon. She paid scrupulous attention to the bacon, in order that she would not fly into a thousand pieces of hurt and fear—and anger.

She didn't really know that she was waiting for Patrick, waiting to see what he would do when he came into the kitchen, until he was there, getting his cup from the cupboard and pouring himself coffee as if nothing in the world were the matter.

She glanced at him and smiled. He smiled back.

Then she turned to the frying pan once more and began forking the now-crisp bacon onto a folded paper towel to drain.

"Who was that on the phone?" she asked, her voice shocking her with its utter nonchalance.

He sipped before he answered. "I don't know. They hung up."

Chapter Fourteen

Hearts, of course, do not really shatter. Regina knew this. But at that moment, knowing beyond any doubt that her husband had just told her a blatant lie, Regina felt her heart doing something terrible.

It was splintering into a million pieces inside her chest. And as her heart did that terrible, impossible thing, she went on forking the bacon out of its bed of hot grease and laying it in even strips upon the folded paper towel.

"Smells good," Patrick said.

"Thank you. Would you wake the girls? The table won't set itself."

"Gina?"

She turned, gave him her brightest smile. "Hmm?"

He looked at her. Then, "Nothing. I'll get them up." And he was gone.

When he returned, he poured himself more coffee and slid into his seat. The girls came plodding in shortly after. Marnie poured the milk and put the napkins around, while Teresa set out the plates and flatware. Soon enough, the eggs and toast were ready. They all sat down to eat.

Patrick finished more quickly than usual, Regina thought. And he didn't linger over his coffee. Within ten minutes of sitting down, he was up and on his way to the garage. And then Teresa was off to help Nellie clean the Sunday school rooms, while Marnie headed out to meet Kenny.

Regina was alone in the house that had been her husband's. The house that had become her house, too, because she had worked hard to make it that way.

Right then, it seemed to be a very quiet house.

With great care, Regina picked up her coffee cup and sipped from it. Very deliberately, she swallowed.

She didn't realize that she was staring blankly into space until her glance caught on the little magnets shaped like fruits on the door of the refrigerator. The magnets held random things. A picture of her family taken that day at Bullfinch Bar by an old man who'd been at the boat dock just before they shoved off. A reminder from the girls' dentist in Arkansas, which Marybeth had forwarded so that Regina wouldn't forget to arrange for their checkups. A list of the school supplies that had to be bought before the next school year began. This week's grocery list.

Things to do. To keep a family going.

Regina blinked.

Then, sucking in a deep breath, she stood. Resolutely, she put one foot in front of the other all the way to the sink, where she started the mundane process of cleaning up after the meal.

The phone rang just as she was putting the last glass in the dishwasher. She hesitated, thinking it would probably either be the phantom caller or Nellie, neither of whom she particularly wanted to deal with right then.

But her hand reached out. She picked it up anyway.

"Hello?"

Silence. A click. And then the drone of the dial tone.

Gently she returned the receiver to its cradle.

She decided to go outside and work in the garden of the other house for a while. She still had tomatoes to gather. And the summer squash needed to be picked, too.

Outside, the day was already warm. Regina, in old jeans and tennis shoes, her hair tied up in a bandanna, set to work, picking vegetables, weeding, nipping dead leaves and pulling out withered stalks.

Her plan was to gradually simplify this garden, have mostly lawn and hardy shrubs back here. It would be easier to care for, when they found a tenant. In the spring, she would plant a new garden at the other house.

If I'm still at the other house.

Regina stifled a little gasp as the awful thought got away from her and reached the conscious levels of her mind.

And then she dropped down onto her bottom in the dirt between the squash rows. She removed her gardening gloves, pushed the sweaty tendrils of hair back from her moist forehead and told herself that she absolutely would not cry.

But she was going to have to confront Patrick. She probably should have confronted him this morning when he lied about Chloe's call. Or even before that. Maybe what she really should have done was to announce her presence on the line when she picked it up and heard Chloe's voice. But instead, she'd quietly hung up.

Lies beget lies, Regina, her mother used to say. And her mother had been right—at least about that. If Patrick chose to lie about a phone conversation with Chloe, that didn't mean that she, Regina, had to lie right along with him.

She had told him when she married him that she would have honesty, above all, in their marriage. Yet this morning, she had been no more honest than he had been.

But tonight, after the girls were safely tucked in their beds, she would have it out with him. She would have the truth from him, about what was going on between him and the woman he claimed he no longer loved.

And after she had the truth, she would decide what to do next.

Regina picked herself up from the ground and beat the dirt from the seat of her jeans with her gardening gloves. She felt better, she decided, now that she knew what she would do.

She glanced at her watch. It was near noon. Soon the girls would be home and wondering where lunch was. Patrick, who sometimes came home for lunch, might be wandering in, too. She ought to go decide what to feed them.

She was just turning for the kitchen door when a flicker of movement at the back fence caught her eye. She stood still, puzzled for a moment, as she registered the fact that someone was looking at her over the fence. And then there was a bumping sound, like a knee hitting one of the boards. After that came a faint rustling noise.

The fine hairs at Regina's nape rose up. "Who is that?"

But no one answered. Swiftly Regina jumped across the rows of squash and pumpkins and the staked tomato vines. She wanted to see the intruder running away. She grabbed two of the fence slats and pulled herself up to peer out over Ebert's Field, a narrow strip of grass and locust trees that ran between Pine Street and the next street over.

"I saw you! I saw you watching me!"

No response came back. The late-summer grass was golden. The locust trees were starting to look parched. Regina could see the bell tower on the church, over on Prospect Street, and the shine of the flagpole over at the school on Gold Run Way. But as for the person who had been watching her, there wasn't a sign.

Perhaps it had been her imagination.

But she knew that wasn't so. She'd seen the crown of a blond head. And before the intruder ducked and jumped down, Regina had caught a quick flash of long, beautifully manicured pink fingernails gripping the fence, fingernails just like Chloe Swan's.

This was too much.

Tonight, when she talked to Patrick, she was going to tell him what she'd seen. She'd find out if he had any better suggestions for her than to pretend like none of this was happening.

If he had suggestions, fine. She'd listen and very likely follow them.

But if not, she would make a few decisions of her own and then act on them. She could confront Chloe, as she planned to confront Patrick. Or she could even call Sheriff Pangborn and tell him what was going on.

She wasn't sure what she'd do yet. But before she went to sleep tonight, she would know, and that was that.

She went inside and took a quick shower to wash off the garden dirt. Then she donned clean clothes and went to the kitchen where she began making sandwiches.

Both girls arrived within minutes of each other. Marnie came first. She had a cut over her eye.

"What happened to you?"

Marnie shrugged. "Nothin'. I fell and whacked myself." She got a look at the can Regina was opening and complained, "Yuck. Tuna. Can't I have PB and J?"

"You had peanut butter and jelly yesterday."

"Yeah, cause I like it. I used to have it every day. Before *you* came along."

"Well, now you have it every *other* day. It's often enough, I think."

"I'm the one who's eatin' it."

"Yes, but I'm the boss. Now please go wash your hands."

Grumbling, Marnie tramped upstairs to the bathroom. She was just reentering the kitchen when Teresa arrived. "I'm home. I'll go wash," the older girl called from the front door.

Regina and Marnie locked glances. Marnie muttered, "I know, I know. Why can't I be more like her?"

"Did I say that?"

"You thought it."

"I most certainly did not. I would not want you to be anyone but Marnie. I like you just the way you are."

Marnie muttered some more and appeared to be trying to keep from smiling. "I'll pour the milk."

"That would be nice. Thank you."

A few minutes later, Teresa came back in. She only had a few minutes, she said, because Alicia Brown and Tammy Rice were going swimming at the long hole and they'd invited her to come too. And the long hole was three miles from town, after all. It took a while to walk there. And it was okay if she went, wasn't it?

Regina nodded and agreed that it certainly was okay. "But be home by five."

Teresa agreed that she would not be late and then ate faster than was probably good for her. She was in her swimsuit, with her shorts and T-shirt thrown over it, and out the door fifteen minutes after she'd first walked in.

Marnie took another bite of tuna sandwich, grimaced, and remarked, "Alicia Brown and Tammy Rice. Yuck."

"What's wrong with Alicia and Tammy?"

"They're a coupla sissies, that's what. But I suppose that's okay with Saint Teresa. She's a sissy herself."

Regina said nothing, only put on an expression that she meant to be noncommittal. She was glad to see that Teresa was rekindling old friendships.

And she was also glad that her stepdaughters had come home for lunch. Fixing their sandwiches and sparring with Marnie had lifted her spirits. That was the good thing about having children, she was finding out. When things seemed out of control, they brought you back down to earth.

"Can I be done now?"

Regina studied Marnie's half-eaten tuna sandwich. "Nothing else until dinner, then."

"Well, what if I get hungry before dinner?"

"Then you'll wish you'd eaten the rest of that sandwich, won't you?"

"Oh, all right." Doggedly, Marnie picked up the remaining half of the sandwich and bit into it. She chewed and swallowed, her face twisted to show her utter loathing of tuna fish. Bite by slow bite, she finished it off, while Regina calmly ate her own sandwich and tried to pretend she didn't notice all the facial contortions.

"There," Marnie said at last. "I'm done. Can I have a cupcake?"

"Fruit first."

"Aw, Gina . . ."

Regina pushed the fruit bowl in Marnie's direction. Scowling, Marnie chose a peach, which she ate with much slurping and grunting. Regina ignored the noises. After all, the peach was quite juicy, and Marnie was careful to use her napkin each time the juice got away from her and dribbled down her stubborn little chin.

"Okay," Marnie said at last, wiping with the napkin one more time. "Now, about that cupcake . . ."

"Yes, you may have one."

"Great." Marnie pushed back her chair and carried her plate and milk glass to the sink. She was just rinsing the plate when the phone rang. She grabbed for the hand towel and quickly dried her hands. "That's Kenny. I know." She picked up the phone. "Hey, Kenny, what's...?" The words died on her lips. "Hello? Hello, who's there?"

And then she turned away, toward the kitchen window and hissed into the phone, "I know who you are. Why don't you just leave us alone, Chloe Swan?" And she slammed the receiver down.

Regina stared at the child's thin back for a moment, wondering what in the world she should do next. Then she stood. "Marnie?"

"I want my cupcake." Without looking at her stepmother, Marnie knelt and opened the doors of the cabinet where the crackers and packaged desserts were kept. She grabbed up the promised treat and straightened.

Regina was waiting for her. "That was Chloe Swan on the phone?"

Marnie clutched her treat and didn't meet Regina's eyes. "I don't know. She didn't talk. She just hung on the line and breathed."

"Has that happened before?"

"Before." Marnie's brows drew together as she pondered the word. "Before, when?"

"In the last few days."

"I don't know. Not for sure. Probably."

"Marnie, what do you mean?"

"I mean, she always just hung up before. But I bet it's been her, when the phone rings and there's no one there."

"Why do you believe the hang-up caller is Chloe?"

"Gina, I gotta get goin'."

"In a minute." Gently, Regina took the girl by the shoulders, turned her around and guided her back to the table.

She sat her down in a chair and knelt before her. "Marnie, why do you think that was Chloe on the phone?"

Marnie pressed her lips together and looked away.

"Please, Marnie. I'm on your side."

"I know. But..."

"Yes?"

"Everybody says..."

"*Who* says?"

"Well, at least Kenny. He said today that he heard his mom and dad talking."

"About what?"

"Gina..."

"Come on, honey. I can't work this out if you won't tell me what it is. What did Kenny hear his mom and dad say?"

Marnie finally looked at Regina. Her blue eyes were moist, but she valiantly held back the tears. Marnie Jones, after all, was no sissy. She lifted her chin. "They said that Chloe Swan's going to take Dad away from you."

Right then, it took all the determination Regina possessed not to flinch and further upset the innocent child. She forced a reassuring smile. And then she declared with a confidence she was a million miles from feeling, "Well, they're wrong."

Marnie turned her head and looked at her stepmother from the corner of her eye. "They are?"

"You'd better believe it."

"You're sure?"

"I am."

"You're... not going to leave us?"

"Absolutely not."

"No matter what happens?"

"No matter what happens." Miraculously, as she made this incredible promise, Regina realized she would do everything in her power to keep it. No matter what happened, she would not desert her stepdaughters. One way or another, she would do what she could to help them grow up. And then the significance of the cut over Marnie's eye dawned on her. "Marnie, did you fight with Kenny over this?"

Marnie scratched at a bug bite on her left knee.

"Marnie."

The child looked up. "Oh, all right. Yeah, I fought with him. And I won, too. But we made up and everything's settled. He won't be dissin my family anymore."

"Dissin?"

"Yeah. Dissin. Disrespecting."

"Oh. I see." Regina drew in a breath and pointed out, "Marnie. Fighting never—"

"I know, I know. Fighting never settled anything. You told me that before. And I know you're right." She scratched her knee again. "But I'm a Jones."

Regina did her best to look stern and forbidding. "That is no excuse."

"I know, and I'll try to do better."

Regina had never seen her younger stepdaughter look so contrite. She was absolutely adorable. Regina had to bite her lip to keep from telling her so.

Marnie was peering at her, narrow-eyed. "Gina, you ain't gonna start kissin' me, are you?"

"Me?" Regina tried to sound surprised at the question.

"Yeah. You got that look you get just before you grab a person and hug them."

Regina put up both hands. "I promise. Hands off." She stood.

And the phone rang again.

The child and the woman looked at each other. Then Regina went to answer. "Hello?"

"Hi, Mrs. Jones. It's Kenny. Can I talk to Marnie?"

"Hold on." Regina held out the phone to her stepdaughter, and mouthed "Kenny" at her.

With the resilience of the child she was, Marnie bounced from the chair, her misery forgotten, and hurried to grab the phone. "Yeah. What? Okay. Hold on." She put her hand over the mouthpiece. "Can I meet him for swimming?"

"Sure."

"Okay. Half hour. See you then." She hung up and grinned at her stepmother. "Well. Gotta go." She turned for the hall to her room.

"Marnie."

Marnie paused in the doorway and looked back. "Yeah?"

"I'll work out this problem."

Marnie nodded. "I know." The look of absolute certainty in her eyes was humbling to Regina. "That Chloe Swan hasn't got a chance," Marnie declared in a confidential whisper. And then she turned and disappeared down the hall.

Regina quickly set about straightening up after their lunch. A few minutes later, Marnie yelled at her from the front door.

"I'm gone!"

"Be back by five!"

"I will. See ya!"

The slamming of the door told Regina that she was alone in the house once more. The girls were safely out of the way.

And Regina was going to do what she should have done earlier. She would talk with Patrick. Now. She was not going to wait until tonight. She'd already waited longer than she should have. And because she had held off, Marnie had suffered. This simply could not go on one moment longer.

Regina picked up the phone to call Patrick at the garage. And then she set it back down. Calling him would only give him another chance to put her off. She was through being put off. She would go over to the garage unannounced and insist that she must have a few minutes alone with him right now.

Regina grabbed the notepad by the phone and scribbled a note to the girls.

> Gone over to the garage for a few minutes. Back soon.
> Love, Gina

Then she went to the bathroom, where she rinsed her face, put on fresh lipstick and combed her hair. On the way out, she stuck the note on the front door.

Chapter Fifteen

Patrick stood behind the parts counter in the office of his garage. He was thumbing through the parts book, looking for the order number for a window regulator on a '79 Trans Am. He was also thinking that he ought to break for lunch soon. His stomach was starting to complain. He wanted food.

He looked up, the order book forgotten for a moment, as he stared blankly out the bank of waist-high windows opposite the counter. The windows flanked the outside door that led to a side parking area.

Right then, Josh Riggins, Kenny's father, strolled by the windows. Josh waved. Patrick lifted his hand and waved back. But it was a mechanical gesture. Patrick hardly saw Josh. He hardly saw anything right then. He was hungry. And he was thinking of Gina.

Hell, whenever he thought of food, or home, comfort or shelter, he thought of Gina. He wanted to go home to her for lunch. But she was testy with him lately. And he was afraid if he went home, she might start in on him about Chloe.

Not that he blamed her for anything she said about Chloe. Chloe was becoming a problem, a problem that wasn't just fading away, as he had originally hoped it might. Chloe was . . . Hell, there was no other way to say it; Chloe was on the rampage.

He knew damn well that the whole town was buzzing over it. Over poor, brokenhearted Chloe and her hopeless love for Patrick Jones. People thought the whole thing was some great high drama, some new Jones legend in the making. Like that old story about his father and mother and Rory Drury that people still couldn't get enough of repeating whenever any one of them was given half a chance.

People didn't seem to realize that what they thought was a great story, was actually his damn *life.* And Regina's. And Marnie's and Tessy's, too.

They saw Chloe, who could be so sweet and look so pretty, and they didn't realize that the woman had a *problem,* for heaven's sake. They felt sorry for her, they sympathized with her. And he understood their urge to do that. Hell, he felt sorry for her himself. But their sympathizing only made her behavior worse.

Chloe Swan had been her daddy's darling and her mama's only girl. Melanie Swan still treated her as if she were a damn princess, clucking over her, petting her, giving her anything she wanted before she even asked for it.

And as a result of this treatment, Chloe had grown up into a woman who only wanted what she couldn't have. Patrick had learned that through hard experience. But he had really believed, the past few months, that he was finally rid of her.

He'd dared to imagine that she might have found happiness with the guy she ran off with. But apparently, Chloe Swan just wasn't in the market for happiness.

When she'd called this morning and demanded that he see her, he'd known things were getting really bad. He'd told her to leave him and his family the hell alone, but he knew that wouldn't hold her off forever.

And then, when he'd come in the kitchen, he'd felt so damn guilty, looking at Gina and knowing her goodness. He hated to see her stuck in the middle of this mess that she'd had no hand in creating.

Now, pondering the way he'd handled it when she asked him who had called, he wondered if he should have told her the truth. But hell, it wasn't his wife's problem. It was his. And one way or another, he was going to solve it on his own.

He shook his head and looked down at the parts book again, thinking he'd find the part and order it and then call over to Lily's Café for a ham on rye. He ran his finger down the page.

And then the door buzzer rang. He looked up.

And into the wide, wounded green eyes of Chloe Swan.

His stomach lurched. Damn, he did not want to deal with this now.

He thought of his mechanics, less than thirty feet away through the shop door. Whatever was said probably wouldn't escape their hearing.

Well, fine. The hell-raiser inside him sneered. *Let 'em hear. Let 'em stare.*

Behind Chloe, the door clicked shut. She leaned against it, her pretty face full of suffering and thwarted longing. She drew in a long, distressed breath.

"Oh, Patrick..." Her voice was purely pathetic. She'd always had that talent for making him feel like a rat. She could make him pity her and despise himself with almost no effort at all. "How could you?"

"How could I what?" he growled.

"You know what." She lifted her chin in affronted suffering. "How could you do that? How could you marry someone else—*again?* At least you had a *reason,* with Marybeth. I mean, since you went and got her pregnant and all. But you had no excuse, none at all, to marry that mousy little nothing, Regina Black."

"Watch what you say about my wife."

She pretended not to hear the warning. "Look, I understand you had a problem." She straightened a little, a noble soul pushed to the end of her rope. "You needed a wife to get your girls. But all you had to do was tell my mother. She would have contacted me and I would have come right back. You know that. It makes no sense. You could have told me what you needed, and I would have been there for you. I would have said yes." Chloe shook her pretty head in disbelief. "You could be married to *me* now...."

After her voice trailed off, he waited a moment before he spoke, just to see if she was going to listen. When she glared and sniffed and held her tongue, he told her, "Next to helping my girls come into the world, marrying Regina Black was the best thing I ever did in my whole useless life."

Chloe gasped. "You can't mean that."

"I do. I mean it. Absolutely."

"But you—"

He'd had enough. He laid it out for her. "There's not a damn thing more to say between you and me, Chloe. It's *over.* It's been over for thirteen years. Wake up. Snap out of it. Get on with your life."

"Oh!" The sound was sharp and full of pain. Her big eyes brimmed. "Oh, no. Oh, Patrick. I *love* you. *She* can't love you like I love you. Oh, when are you going to see that? Nobody can love you like I do."

All at once, he felt very tired. It was always like this when he was finally forced to deal with this woman. He felt rotten, and then fed up. And then very, very tired. "Look, Chloe..."

She straightened from her slumped pose against the door. "No. I won't look. *You* look." She started walking toward him, across the small space to the counter, then around the end.

"Chloe." He said her name as a warning to stay away.

But Chloe never heeded warnings. Suddenly she was flying at him, her arms outstretched. "I love you. You love me. Hold me, darling. Kiss me, please." She came at him like a bullet.

"Damn it, Chloe!"

She landed with a thud against his chest and wrapped her clutching arms around his neck. "Kiss me, darling. Love me, please." She shoved her mouth up under his. He was trying to peel her off him, and he looked down at her to tell her to let go. But looking down was a mistake, because she managed to get a liplock on him that wouldn't quit.

Right then, the damn door buzzer sounded.

"Oh!" He heard Regina's sharp gasp.

He tore his mouth off of Chloe's and looked into his wife's bewildered gray eyes. "Gina!"

"Patrick?" She blinked.

"Gina, I—"

And then, without another sound, Regina turned and fled.

"Good. Let her go." Chloe pressed her breasts against him.

He reached back and gripped her wrists and peeled her off of his body.

She tried to grab for him again. "Patrick!"

He slid out of her way. Just then Zeb Wilbur, one of his mechanics, came in through the shop door. "Hey, Patrick, what about that—"

Patrick didn't wait for the rest of the question. "Keep an eye on things, Zeb," he barked over his shoulder as he rushed for the door.

Behind him, Chloe went on pleading. "No, wait. Let her go, Patrick. I'm here for you. I love you. I—"

But Patrick was already out the door.

When he got to the street, he looked both ways, and then caught sight of Regina half a block up, walking fast, approaching the turn onto Pine Street.

He shouted, "Regina! Get back here!"

But all she did was start to run.

He broke into a sprint himself. Damned if she was going to run away from him.

"Regina!"

She sped around the corner.

He raced up the street, paying no attention to Rocky Collins, who turned to gape after him, shaking his head. He didn't even spare a glance for Tondalaya Clark, except to mutter a low "Sorry," when he almost ran her down. And as for Tyler Conley and Betty Brown, who just happened to be strolling down Main Street right then, well, he didn't even notice them.

But they noticed him. And they understood that those crazy Joneses were at it again.

"Regina! I'm serious as a terminal disease here. Don't you run from me, damn you!" He made the corner and dashed around it, his powerful legs pumping as fast as they would go. "Regina!"

But she had a good start on him, and she was surprisingly swift. She fled down the street toward their two houses, not wasting a moment with backward glances that might have given him enough of an edge to catch up.

He hoped she would turn into her house, because it was kept locked and if she had to fumble with a key, it would give him the edge he needed.

But no such luck. She tore right past that gate, and flung back the gate of the house they shared, not even wasting the second it would have taken to close it behind her. She pounded up the walk, took the steps in one leap and ran in the door.

That she took the time to slam. In his face. He was up the porch steps and had grabbed the handle just as he heard the dead bolt shoot home.

He swore, words that would have had Marnie consigned to her room on bread and water for a week. And then, since he'd left the garage without his keys, he beat his fist against the ungiving wood.

"Regina! Let me in! Damn you, you'd better let me in, or when I get my hands on you..." He let the threat trail off, incapable at that moment of thinking of anything sufficiently gruesome to describe what he would do to her once he could get to her.

"Regina!" He pounded some more, a sharp volley of blows, then a series of hard, separate thuds. As he pounded, he shouted her name. A piece of paper, a note for the girls, was in his way. He ripped it off the door and tore it to shreds.

He pounded some more.

And then, still pounding, he admitted to himself that she wasn't going to let him in just because he yelled and beat on the door.

He stopped pounding and looked around him, trying to decide what he should do next. He noted that, across the street, old Mrs. Quail was sitting in her porch rocker watching him. But he didn't really care. His wife had locked him out and he wanted in. That was all he cared about right then.

He seriously began considering his options, and found himself wondering if Regina might have kept on going, out the back door. Could she, at this very minute, be darting through Ebert's Field toward Gold Run Way?

He really would find some horrible way to get even with her if she'd done that, he vowed. But then, the more he thought about it, he doubted she'd run out the back. She'd wanted shelter—from him. And now, in his house, with his own front door locked against him, she probably assumed she'd found it.

Hah! he thought furiously. Who the hell did she think she was dealing with here? She should have married that twit Marcus, if she wanted a man she could get away from.

What she *had* done was marry a Jones, and a Jones was inescapable. Everyone knew that.

The question of the moment was, should he bust in the door?

He shook his head. He wasn't ready to go that far. Yet.

He began pacing the perimeter of the house, checking for open windows where all he'd have to do was pry off a screen to get inside. He found none. When he got to the back door, he tested it and found it locked.

His temper rose again as he realized she was one step ahead of him. While he'd been making a satisfying but pointless racket beating on the front door, she'd quietly gone around and locked the back door and shut all the windows.

She'd always been more coolheaded than he was. It was one of the hundred and one things he admired the hell out of her for—under ordinary circumstances. Now, however, it just made him madder than he already was.

He told himself to be calm. And then he walked around the house again, looking up at the second story this time. She'd shut and locked all of the windows up there against him, too. Except, he saw by squinting and shielding his eyes, for the window at the back of the walk-in closet in their bedroom. It was a window that opened from a top hinge; it swung up and then could be held ajar by a locking side brace. In that one small window, he couldn't see the shine of glass panes behind the screen. That meant she hadn't thought to go in the closet and latch it down.

It was maybe two feet square. Plenty of room for a determined man to wiggle through.

A cold smile curled his lips.

He quietly walked to the front of the house again, paying no mind when he saw that Mrs. Quail was still on her porch and had been joined by her nosy old husband, Ben.

Patrick sat down on the step and took off his boots and socks. Then, his feet bare, he jumped to the porch railing and shimmied up one of the posts that supported the porch roof.

Silent as a snake in new grass, he hoisted himself onto the porch roof, tiptoed across it and then managed to boost himself onto the roof of the house. Cautiously, he worked his way around the roof, watching his step and doing his best to make no sound. At last he reached the spot he was seeking, right above the little closet window. There, he stretched out on his stomach and hung his torso over the roof's edge.

With only a minimum of whispered cursing, he managed to pry the screen off and toss it to the lawn below, where it landed with a barely distinguishable thud. Then he slid around, until he could hang his legs over the edge. He scooted backward, keeping his torso on the roof and feeling with his feet until he found the windowsill.

Piece of cake, he thought with grim triumph, as he slid beneath the braced-up window and into the closet that was lined with his clothes on one side and Regina's on the other. His bare feet found the floor and he landed in a slight crouch. Then he straightened.

In three steps he was at the door that opened onto the bedroom he shared with his wife. He stuck out a hand and pushed it wide.

"Oh!" Regina jumped from the edge of the bed and backed toward the nightstand. "Patrick!" Her pale, long-fingered hand flew to her throat. "What are you doing here?"

He leaned against the jamb and folded his arms across his chest. "I live here. Remember?"

Her breathing was agitated. She forced herself to lower her hand from her throat and drop it to her side. She probably thought she looked calmer that way. But it only gave him a clear view of the frantic pulse that beat against the white skin where her hand had been. "How did you—?"

"You forgot to lock the closet window." He shook a finger at her. "Not very smart. Where are the kids?"

"Gone for the rest of the day. Thank goodness." She yanked her shoulders back, to show him how unafraid of him she was. "And I do not want to talk with you." She started for the door.

He sidestepped and blocked her path. "Don't try it."

"Move out of my way, please."

He gave her a little nudge toward the bed. "Sit down."

She didn't move, only narrowed those eyes of hers at him, tipped her head back and looked down that slim, finely shaped nose. "Please do not touch me. And I said I do not wish to speak with you right now."

"I heard you."

"Well, then—"

"And I don't give a good damn about what you *wish*. You'll speak with me, all right. And you'll do it now."

The fine nostrils quivered in outrage. "You . . . you . . ."

"Me, me *what?*"

She whirled away from him and went to the rocker by the window, where she plunked herself down and began wrathfully to rock back and forth. She looked out the window, a flat, unseeing kind of look, and pretended that he wasn't even there.

He bore about thirty seconds of that. Then he marched right over to her and stopped the infernal rocking by grabbing the chair arms.

"Let go," she said, still looking out the window at nothing.

"No."

She grimaced, as she tried to force the chair to rock, in spite of the fact that he was holding it still. And then, when she got nowhere, she started kicking. Her feet flailed furiously. She got him a good one right in the shin.

He swore roundly, and then he grabbed for her.

"Don't you touch me, you bully! You let me alone!" She kicked and pounded at him, as he carried her to the bed and tossed her, like a sack of meal, across it. Then he came down on top of her, pinning her arms above her head with his hands and holding her body in place with his own. All the while she railed at him.

"I hate you, you rotten, insufferable, awful man! I hate you. Let me go. Let me go. Let me go!"

He held her, grim and determined, now that he had her down and pinned, until she finally wore down a little. With a low moan she turned her head to the side and pressed her eyes closed.

"Look at me."

"Never."

"You're acting like one of the girls, for goodness sake. Having a damn fit because—"

"Because you *betrayed* me." She did look at him then. And if looks could do physical damage, he would have been charred to a cinder right there and then.

"I did *not* betray you." He was trying his damnedest to keep his temper. But he was not a calm man by nature and she was getting pretty carried away with this, running up Main Street to get away from him, locking him out of the house, refusing even to speak with him and then actually kicking him in the shin over there at the rocking chair. She was usually a reasonable woman, but about this, she wasn't giving a single inch.

She struggled again, an impatient, hopeless kind of wriggling, her face all twisted up with frustration and rage. And then her slim body went limp beneath him.

Their eyes met and locked.

"If I let you up, will you quit trying to get away?"

She didn't answer, only glared at him.

"Are you ready to listen to what I have to say?" He asked the question between clenched teeth.

"What is there to say, Patrick?" The words were spoken in that Sunday school teacher voice she could put on whenever she wanted to make a man feel like a worm.

"There's a hell of a lot to say, and you know it."

"Oh, do I?"

"Damn right."

"Well, if there is a lot to say, I certainly have no idea what it is. I think what you've *done* just about says it all."

"I didn't do a damn thing."

"Well." She raised her nose so high, she was lucky it didn't disappear into her hair. "I suppose you *would* say that."

"Because it's true."

Her lips pulled back in a she-wolf's snarl. Damn, she had a mean side to her. Who the hell would have thought it? That sickly little Regina Black could be mean as a she-wolf when she thought her man had cheated on her.

Which he hadn't. And which he was going to tell her, if only she'd give him half a chance.

But she wasn't giving any chances.

He pointed out, "When you invited Marcus Shelby into my house, I settled down enough to listen to your explanation of why you'd done it."

"That was different."

"How?"

She rolled her eyes, as if the answer were so obvious there was no need to say it. "You knew I didn't care for Marcus. I told you so."

"And I told you I don't love Chloe Swan."

"It's not the same."

"It damn well is."

"It isn't." She dragged in a fuming breath. "I know who it was on the phone this morning." Her voice was as cold as a witch's caress. "It was Chloe. And yet you lied to my face and said the person hung up before you found out who it was."

"All right," he admitted. "I shouldn't have lied. But I only did it because I didn't want you to worry, not because there was anything going on between me and that woman."

"Oh, stop it. She called you this morning and you lied to me about it. And then, just now I saw you kissing her."

"The hell you did. You saw *her* kissing me. There *is* a damn difference."

"Don't you split hairs with me. That was your mouth and her mouth and there was no space between them. You have cheated on me, Patrick."

"I have not. I—"

"And I simply do not know if I can stay married to you."

When she said that, his heart stopped for a moment. He stared at her, his mouth open. And then he snapped it shut. "What the hell did you say?"

"I said, I don't know if I can—"

He decided he didn't really want to hear it again. "Don't." He snarled the word. And then he jumped backward, away from her. He didn't even want to touch her right then. When he was on his feet he glowered down at her, where she lay, still stretched on her back across the bed. "Don't say the rest of it. I don't want to hear it. There are a lot of things I always thought highly of you for, Regina. And two of them are your fairness and the fact that you aren't a quitter. But you're not being fair now. You've judged and convicted me of a thing I've always sworn to you I would never do. And you've made your judgment without even listening when I tried to tell you my side of it."

She looked just a little ashamed, but she still wasn't going to be fair. "I know what I heard. And what I saw."

He stared at her, a look he meant to burn right through her. Then he said softly, "You don't trust me worth a damn."

"I—"

He threw up a hand. She fell silent. He went on. "But worse than that, worse that judging me unfairly and having not one bit of trust in me, you dare to tell me you might not stay married to me. That's the biggest bunch of bunk I've ever heard. I've kept my word to you. I've been true to you. And you can bet that piano of yours that you'll stay married to me. Finally, after half a lifetime, I managed to find me a decent wife. And I'll be damned if I'll ever let you go."

She let out a sharp, outraged cry when he said that, and scuttled back on the bed. She glared at him, her eyes like two pieces of hard coal.

And then, out of nowhere, she was shouting, "A decent wife! That's what I am to you, *all* I am to you. Someone to mother your children and cook your meals and clean your house. But you have to go somewhere else when it comes to love and passion. I can see that now. I can understand that now."

He gaped at her. And then his temper, held by a slender thread for so long, snapped free. "What the hell are you talking about? *Where* else have I been? I've been here, with you. And you damn well know it, too."

He stared down at her, wanting to grab her and shake her until she admitted the truth. That he *was* a true husband. And that his passion, like the sweat of his brow and the work of his hands, like his laughter and his sorrow, was hers, only hers.

The urge to grab her, though, was a violent urge. He dared not give in to it.

So rather than reach for her in his rage, he spun on his heel and stomped out of the room.

He heard her call his name when he was halfway down the stairs. But he didn't turn. He didn't pause. He pounded the rest of the way down the stairs and out the door, only pausing to scoop up his boots and socks before he headed for the front gate.

Chapter Sixteen

Five minutes after she heard the front door slam, Regina was still sitting on the bed. She was staring blindly at the rocking chair by the window.

And she was feeling deeply ashamed.

Patrick had been right. She had judged and convicted him without listening at all when he tried to tell his side of things. But she hadn't wanted to hear his side of things. She had seen Chloe Swan in his arms, and all logical thought had fled.

By the bed, the phone started ringing. Regina shifted her dazed glance to look at it. She didn't want to answer it. But there was an off chance the call might concern the girls. So with a sigh she reached over and picked it up.

"Oh, my sweet heaven. Regina, is that you?"

"What is it, Nellie?" Regina thought with disinterest that her voice sounded as lifeless as she felt.

"Has he hurt you? Everyone saw him chasing you down the street. And heard him beating on your door. And then Mrs. Quail says he climbed up on the *roof*, to get to you. Are you all right?"

"I'm fine, Nellie."

"You stay right there. I'll be right over."

"No."

"Excuse me?"

"I said no. I don't want any company right now."

"But, my dear, if you—"

"I mean it, Nellie. I want to be left alone now."

"Well, I declare I never—"

"Goodbye, Nellie." Regina hung up.

She sat for another few moments, hating herself in a list-less kind of way. And then she slid off the bed and went to the bathroom, where she rinsed her face and took two aspirin in an effort to quell the headache that was beginning to pound behind her eyes.

Once again, after she'd taken the aspirin, she found herself staring blindly into space. This time she was standing at the bathroom mirror, holding her water glass and gaping at her own lackluster reflection.

Where could he have gone? she wondered. She was worried about him. He could be a very angry man sometimes. But she'd never seen him *that* angry before. Would he do something crazy, being that mad?

He probably would, she realized with a low moan. She just hoped he wouldn't hurt anyone—especially not himself.

Maybe she should call around town. Track him down.

No. She shook her head. She would leave him alone for a while. He needed some time on his own to cool down.

He'd be home when he'd gotten the rage out of his system. And then they would talk.

She made a face at the thought of the things he would be likely to say to her, even after he had cooled down. She hated to admit that she probably deserved whatever he would choose to say.

There was just no more escaping the truth. She'd behaved abominably. And she knew exactly what had brought her to this pass.

It was the fiery love she bore him that she had never revealed. It was her foolish pride, that wouldn't let her admit to him what she really wanted from him.

There was a strong thread of selfishness in her, she was forced to admit now. She was not only the giving, patient Christian woman her mother had raised her to be. She was also like the mountain lion she had faced down when she was five years old, and like Patrick. She had a deep streak of the feral within her.

She did not believe Patrick had betrayed her. She had never believed it. She had believed *him* when he had said that he was a Jones and a Jones doesn't cheat. But seeing him with Chloe's arms around him had stirred up her secret rage at what she'd never had from him.

He'd been a good and true husband. All he had was hers. Except his love.

And she wanted that. She wanted his heart. She wanted it *all*.

She'd been telling herself since the day after she married him that she could do without his love as long as he was true to her. But that had been a lie.

And lies beget lies.

Regina shook herself. She thought of her daughters, not even realizing that she now considered them as much hers as children of her own body might have been.

Soon enough, the girls would be home. And they mustn't see her looking frantic. They were both bright. They would probably sense that all was not well.

Regina believed that a parent had a duty to show her children by example how one coped with trouble. Children needed to be able to trust the adults who cared for them, to know they could count on their elders to face difficulties with restraint and fortitude.

Thank heaven they had not been home to observe her appalling behavior a little while ago. She had little doubt that they would eventually hear about how their father had chased their stepmother down the street. Half the town, after all, had witnessed that. And some talkative soul would be sure to end up telling them all about it. But at least they'd been spared having to witness it firsthand.

By rote, Regina pulled the pins from her tumbled, tangled hair. She brushed the brown strands with even strokes, and then pinned it back in place. She applied blusher on her pale cheeks and fresh color to her lips. After that she forced a smile for her face in the mirror.

It was a rather bleak smile, she decided. But it would simply have to do.

She went out to the kitchen, to get started on the lasagna she'd planned to make for dinner. She prepared the sauce, and ground up the three kinds of sausage she liked to use. She cooked the pasta. And then she layered the casserole, slowly, carefully, as if by concentrating on preparing a nice dinner she might make up for the way she'd behaved not too long before.

When the lasagna was ready, it was still too early to actually start baking it. So she prepared the garlic bread ahead, so it would also be ready to stick in the oven when the time came. By then it was three.

She went to the phone and stared at it, longing to pick it up and make a few calls. She could call Delilah, or Eden. She could ask them if they knew where her husband was.

But then she remembered her resolve to give him time to himself. She would not further upset him by chasing him all over town.

Right then, the phone she was staring at began to ring. Regina gasped and jumped back as she felt the goose bumps break out on her skin. It was eerie, to have it ringing like that, as if her watching it had made it happen.

And Regina *knew* who it would be. The phantom caller. Chloe.

Yes, Chloe. Since the incident in the backyard before lunch, she had no doubt in her mind that Chloe and the phantom were one and the same.

The phone rang a second time. Regina reached out a hesitant hand and then pulled it back.

The kitchen phone was also an answering machine. There was no reason she shouldn't wait and let the machine take the call. She could stand right here and listen, and pick up if it was Patrick or one of the girls.

That's what she should do, she knew it.

The phone rang again. One more ring, and the machine would take over. If she could just wait until—

The fourth ring shrilled out.

And Regina's hand grabbed the receiver from its cradle in midring.

"Hello?"

Silence.

"Hello. Who's there?"

And then Chloe spoke. "Let him go, Regina. He's mine. He's always been mine."

A thousand emotions roiled inside of Regina. Relief that at last Chloe was willing to speak. Anger at the way her family had been victimized by all this. Frustration at the unfairness of it. And fear, too. Chloe seemed to have really gone over the edge lately. Who knew what she might do?

"Let Patrick go," Chloe said again.

Regina wanted to shout out a few demands and accusations of her own. But she didn't. Instead, she made herself silently count to three before she spoke.

"This is harassment, Chloe." She took great care to keep her voice calm and rational. "I want your word that you will stop this now, leave me and my family alone, or I will call Sheriff Pangborn as soon as I'm through talking to you."

From the other end of the line, there was a long, quivering indrawn breath. "You don't scare me. You don't scare me one bit. You're nothing, nothing to him, except someone to help him keep his kids. But he loves me. He wants me. You'll never keep a man like him. Face it. And let him go."

"Chloe, I meant what I said. I'm calling the sheriff."

A barrage of passionate curses exploded in Regina's ear. She quietly disconnected the phone.

And then she left the phone off the hook while she found the number of the sheriff's station, which she immediately dialed.

The deputy on duty was Don Brown. Regina asked if she could speak with Sheriff Pangborn, whom she knew better than Deputy Brown.

"I'm sorry, Mrs. Jones," the deputy said. "The sheriff isn't in right now. Why don't you tell me your problem?"

Embarrassed but determined, she told him about what had happened at the post office as well as the incident in the backyard of the other house. She listed the hang-up calls and outlined the gist of the call she'd just received from Chloe.

When she was finished, Deputy Brown advised, "Generally, it's our experience that things like this just blow over, if allowed to run their natural course."

Regina was already regretting having dialed the sheriff's station. What, reasonably, could she expect them to do at this point? She thanked the deputy and hung up, feeling foolish.

She looked at the clock; it was 3:25. She wondered vaguely if time had ever before moved so slowly as it seemed to be doing this particular afternoon.

The phone rang again. This time she let it ring. The machine picked it up and by the time the beep sounded, there was no one on the line.

Regina decided to bake brownies. Anything, to make the time go by faster.

The brownies were in the oven and there was only ten minutes left on the timer when Teresa came in.

"I'm home." Teresa breezed into the kitchen, her skin pink from an afternoon in the sun. She looked as if she didn't have a care in the world. Apparently, no one had told her about the incident this afternoon.

"Mmm. Smells great in here."

Regina forced herself to act as if everything were as it should be. "How was swimming?"

"Great. But I'm covered with sunblock and sand. Can I take my shower now?"

"Go ahead."

Teresa disappeared to clean up. She was downstairs again cutting up the dinner salad when Marnie came in. Like Teresa, Marnie seemed happy and carefree. She must not have heard what had happened, either. Also like her sister, Marnie looked as if she could use a shower. But it was not in her nature to volunteer for such unpleasantness.

When Marnie started to poke a finger in the pan of cooling brownies, Regina shot her a quelling look.

"Go upstairs and wash those hands."

Marnie groaned in protest, and then flounced off to do as she'd been told. When she came back down she set the table.

By then, it was five-thirty and the lasagna and garlic bread were hot and fragrant and ready to eat.

"Where's Dad?" Marnie wanted to know.

"Well, he may be a little late tonight," Regina said, as offhandedly as she could. "Why don't we just sit down without him?"

Marnie and Teresa exchanged a look. Regina realized that she had not sounded as offhand as she'd intended.

But Teresa said, "Sure. I'm starved."

As they took their seats and the meal began, Regina was poignantly aware of the empty space at the head of the table. And from the pensive expressions she observed on the two young faces, so were her daughters. Dinner was mostly a silent affair, punctuated by fits and starts of carefully inane conversation.

Once, just before Marnie cleared off the dinner plates and Teresa brought over the pan of brownies for Regina to cut, the phone rang.

"I'll get it." Teresa stood.

"No." Regina kept her tone very calm. "Let's just let the machine take it. And see who it is first."

Teresa looked bewildered. But she waited as Regina had requested, until the ringing stopped and the recorded message had played. When the beep sounded, there was no one on the other end.

Teresa sank into her chair once more.

Regina felt some explanation was in order. "You both know how we keep getting all those hang-up calls, right?"

Solemnly, both girls nodded.

"Well, I think whoever it is might become discouraged if the machine answers instead of us, that's all. And of course, if it's someone who really wants to talk with any of us, they'll stay on the line and say who they are. Then we can answer."

Both girls agreed that this was a good plan. Regina waited for Marnie to say something about the call she'd taken from Chloe Swan at lunchtime. But Marnie said nothing; she only looked at her stepmother through worried blue eyes.

"Marnie? Is something bothering you?"

Marnie's gaze slid away. "Yeah." She looked back and grinned. "Can I have three brownies, instead of just two?"

"You are a dreamer, my dear."

Marnie shrugged. "Just thought I'd try."

After the brownies were served and eaten, the girls got up and did the dishes smoothly and efficiently. They neither complained nor bickered between themselves.

For the first time since they'd come to live with her and Patrick, Regina found herself longing to hear their arguing voices. A little quarreling on this particular evening would have meant that all was right with their world.

After the dishes were done, Marnie said, "I think I'll go take my bath now."

"Good idea," Regina said, and wanted to cry. The day Marnie went to bathe without coercion was a dark day indeed.

Marnie disappeared upstairs and came down a half an hour later, dressed in her pajamas. "Can we watch some TV?"

Regina was seated in an easy chair crocheting an extra set of coasters that she really didn't need. She looked up over the rim of the glasses she wore for reading and for close work. "Sure. But not too loud."

Marnie flipped on the television and she and Teresa sat at either end of the couch. Two and a half hours crept by to the sounds of sitcom laugh tracks.

"Okay, you two. Bedtime," Regina announced at nine-thirty.

With only minimal grumbling, the girls turned off the television and went to brush their teeth. A few minutes after they'd headed for the bathroom, Marnie returned.

Regina looked up from the afghan she'd started on when she finished the coasters. "What is it, honey?"

Marnie clasped her small hands together and bit her lip. "I know getting tucked in is mostly for babies, and Saint Teresa and me are kinda too big for it . . ."

"Yes?"

"But maybe just tonight, you could do it anyway. Okay?"

Regina removed her glasses and rubbed the bridge of her nose. "I think that's a lovely idea. Go on up and I'll be there in just a minute."

She went to Marnie's room first, where she had to be careful not to walk on the little plastic construction-set pieces that were strewn on the floor. In spite of her care, however, she stepped on something that made a loud crunch.

Out of the darkness, she heard Marnie's sigh. "It's all right, Gina. I prob'ly got two of those anyway."

Regina found the edge of the bed at last. She sat, her eyes slowly becoming adjusted to the darkness of the room. "Tomorrow you'll clean up all those pieces."

"I will, I promise. But now, I guess, since you're here, I'll have to say my prayers."

Regina smiled. "Yes, I'd like that."

"Well. Okay, then." Marnie pressed her eyes closed. "Our Father, who art in heaven . . ."

Marnie murmured the Lord's Prayer in a soft little sing-song, adding at the end, "And bless my dad and Regina and help them to work their problems all out. Amen."

"Amen," Regina agreed.

"You meant what you said today, didn't you, Gina?" Marnie asked then. "About taking care of that problem and not leaving us?"

"I most certainly did." She bent to place a kiss on Marnie's forehead. "Good night, honey."

"'Night, Gina." Marnie turned over and cuddled up into a ball.

Regina rose and carefully picked her way through the debris to the door.

She found Teresa sitting on her bed, her lamp still on, her hands folded in her lap.

"Gina, we must talk."

Quietly Regina closed the door behind her and sat beside her older stepdaughter. "All right."

Teresa spoke with great gravity. "Where is my father?"

"Well, Teresa. I really don't know."

"Did something . . . happen, between you and him?"

Regina nodded. "Yes. We had an argument."

"A bad one?"

"Bad enough. I behaved horribly. Your father was very angry at me. So he left."

Teresa looked disbelieving. "*You* behaved horribly?"

"Yes, I did. Please don't ask me for details, though. I really don't want to explain."

Now Teresa looked extremely knowing. Sagaciously, she nodded. "I understand." Then, suddenly, she was a worried twelve-year-old again. "Did he say when he'd be back?"

"No, he didn't."

Teresa took Regina's hand. "Well, he always does come back. Sooner or later. Please believe me."

"I do believe you. Your father's a good man, with a lot on his mind. Of course he'll be back."

"And when he does, he'll be sorry for whatever he did."

"Teresa, I told you, I was the one who—"

"Whatever. Just please don't give up on him."

"I won't."

"Or... on us."

"Never." Regina wrapped her arm around Teresa and gave a squeeze.

The girl laid her head on Regina's shoulder. "Since we got you, everything is so much better, Gina," she said in a broken little whisper. "It would be awful if you weren't here."

"I'll always be here as long as you need me. One way or another. I promise you." She smoothed the fine blond hair back from Teresa's forehead and placed a kiss there. "Now, into bed."

Regina busied herself pulling back the covers. Teresa slipped between the sheets and Regina pulled them up and tucked them around her.

"Good night, sweetheart," she whispered, and kissed Teresa once more.

She moved softly to the door.

"Gina?"

"Yes?"

"I love you, Gina."

"And I love you."

Regina returned to the living room, where the clock on the mantel was just striking ten. She picked up the beginnings of the afghan and then set it aside again.

She was tired of keeping busy, of pretending she was doing something useful so that she wouldn't have to admit that what she really was doing was waiting.

For her husband to come home.

With a long sigh, Regina switched off the lamps and sat down in the easy chair in the dark. She stared out the window at the streetlight across the way, waiting for Patrick and some resolution to this awful situation.

She had waited nearly an hour when the phone rang. She reached for it by rote, putting it to her ear before she remembered her decision to screen all her calls.

"Hello? Regina? Regina, is that you?"

Regina cleared her throat. *"Marcus?"*

"Yes, Regina. It's me."

Regina was in no mood to deal with an old beau. "Marcus, I really—"

"I know, I know. My calling makes you uncomfortable, and I understand that."

"Okay. If you know this makes me uncomfortable, then why are you calling?"

"Because..." Now it was Marcus's turn to cough. "I, um... Angie and I... Did you know I've been dating Angie?"

Remembering Marcus's singing the other day, Regina actually felt the ghost of a smile on her lips. "Yes. I think I heard that you two were dating."

"Yes, we are." Did bliss have a sound? If it did, it was there in Marcus Shelby's voice right then. Regina was happy for him and for Angie Leslie—at the same time as she felt a little stab of selfish envy that she and Patrick weren't doing as well. Marcus continued, "Angie and I are *together.* And tonight, we went to the Mercantile Grill, and then afterward we stopped in next door at the Hole in the Wall to have a drink. We just left there, actually."

"And?"

"And your husband is there."

"Oh."

"He's drunk and getting drunker. I think what he really wants is for his wife to come and take him home."

"How do you know what my husband wants, Marcus?"

Marcus Shelby snorted. "Oh, come on. Isn't it obvious? That man was after you from that first day when I walked you home from church and he was standing in his yard flexing all those muscles he's got. Why do you think I was always trying to keep you away from him? He's totally in love with you."

"But, Marcus," Regina argued, thoroughly confused, "you came to see me to tell me he *didn't* love me, that he only married me to get his girls."

"Well, of course I said that." Marcus's tone was faintly exasperated. "And I did my best to believe it, too. After all, you had thrown me over for him. My wounded ego wanted revenge. But deep down, I knew that man was crazy about you. The truth was, I never had a chance against the passion between the two of you." From somewhere on Marcus's end of the line, there came a husky feminine laugh. Regina realized that Marcus was not alone. "And it worked out fine, that I lost out," Marcus added in his blissful voice. "Because I found my *own* passion."

Regina didn't quite know what to say. "I see."

"Yes, well. Angie and I thought you might like to know where your husband was."

"I appreciate that."

"No problem. And all the best to you, Regina."

"Thank you, Marcus. Um, same to you."

Regina heard another soft woman's laugh, and then the line was disconnected. Slowly she, too, hung up.

She sat for a few minutes more, considering. And then she decided to take Marcus's advice.

But what to do about the girls?

It took only a moment for Regina to decide. She dialed Delilah Fletcher's number. She was in luck—Delilah answered.

"Hello?"

"Hello, Delilah? This is Regina. Did I wake you?"

"No."

"Delilah, I really need your help."

"Why did I know you were going to say that?"

"I know it's an imposition—"

"No, it's not. It's just inevitable."

"It is?"

"Certainly."

Regina was quite bewildered. "You seem to be way ahead of me on this."

"Of course I am. I've been waiting to hear from you, ever since Nellie called."

"Nellie called you about what happened between Patrick and me?"

"She certainly did."

"I suppose she's calling everyone."

"No doubt. Nellie is such a jewel." Delilah's voice dripped irony. "But don't worry about Nellie. She doesn't have much use for men, so she's never happy when someone she likes gets married. But eventually, she'll grow accustomed to what's happened and she'll stop driving you crazy. I promise."

"I hope you're right."

"I usually am. Now, you need me to help in some way. Correct?"

"Yes, I—"

"All right. What can I do?"

"Well, I want to go over to the Hole in the Wall for a few minutes. I understand that Patrick is there. The girls are in bed, but I hate to leave them alone. I don't want to wake them and upset them, but if they woke and found I was gone, then they would—"

Delilah cut to the point. "How about if I sit with them, until you return?"

"Yes. That's exactly what I—"

"I'll be right there."

"Thank you, I—"

But her sister-in-law had already hung up.

Delilah arrived ten minutes later.

"Thank you, Delilah," Regina said just before she went out the door.

Delilah waved a hand. "What's a family for, anyway? Go on. Get your husband."

"I will."

"And don't let him give you any lip, either."

Regina forced a smile. "I won't." She stepped out into the night as Delilah shut the door.

Regina took her car, so she reached Main Street within minutes of leaving the house.

That late on a weeknight, Main Street was a very quiet place. All the stores were dark. Even the Mercantile Grill had closed for the evening. But of course, the lights at the Hole in the Wall still burned.

Regina easily found a space across from the bar and pulled into it. She got out of the car and hurried across the street.

At the double doors to the saloon, she paused. Entering a bar to find an intoxicated husband was not high on her list of fun things to do. She bolstered her courage by drawing a long breath and squaring her shoulders.

It was then that she heard Patrick's voice, muffled by the doors, coming from inside.

Cautiously, she pushed the doors open, slipped through and slid into the shadows to the right of the doors. Once there, she didn't want to go any farther.

And no one seemed to notice her anyway. They were all looking at Patrick, who was standing on a table in the center of the room, clutching a bottle of whiskey and, it appeared, making some sort of speech.

He proposed grandly, "So I ask you, what's the most important thing, 'tween a husband and wife?"

Around the room, the patrons mumbled to each other. Old Oggie, sitting the next table over from the one his son was standing on, made a disgusted noise in his throat.

Then some fellow Regina didn't know suggested something uncouth.

Several men burst into crude laughter.

Patrick looked down at them, his expression woozy and wounded.

"Pipe down, you animals," Rocky Collins advised. "The man's got something to say."

Patrick scratched his head and looked puzzled. "Er, where was I?"

"The most important thing between a husband and wife," Rocky thoughtfully provided.

"Oh. Yeah. Right." Patrick swayed on his feet. The table he was standing on creaked in protest.

Jared, behind the bar, suggested quietly, "Patrick if you break that table, Eden'll have my hide."

"I'm not gonna break anything." Patrick helped himself to another swig from his bottle, then solemnly declared, "It's come to me. I remember."

"Don't keep us in suspense." The unknown voice was weighted with sarcasm.

"It's *trust!*" Patrick announced with a proud, dazed smile. "Yes, *trust.* Trust is it. Trust is everything."

Regina stared at him, despising herself. He was absolutely right—no matter how much trouble he'd had remembering the word. Trust *was* everything. And she had been guilty of the most appalling lack of it.

And now she was acting like a coward, hiding in the shadows instead of stepping up and telling him she'd been wrong. She forced herself to move out into the light.

Jared saw her. "About time," he muttered.

On the table, Patrick continued, "*Trust,* that's the thing. If you haven't got it, you haven't got what it takes to make it through the rough times. And that's why there oughtta be something about it in the weddin' vows. I'm *serious.* You got your love, your honor and your cherish. But where the hell is your *trust?* And what have you got without it, but a fair-weather kind of thing? And you should never marry a person you can't trust. 'Cause if you don't trust the one you married, then what's it worth? What's it matter?"

Regina, who stood at his feet now, spoke with quiet force. "Patrick."

"Huh?" He looked down and saw her. Then he blinked and squinted. "Gina, honey. S'that really you?"

"Yes. It's me. And I'm sorry I didn't trust you. I truly am."

He went on staring at her, his handsome face flushed with drink—and frank emotion. His expression was one of longing—and of joy. There was no doubt about it. The man was *very* happy to see her. Why, the way he was gazing at her, anyone would think he was crazy in love with her.

Regina's heart seemed to expand in her chest. Could she have been wrong about his feelings all this time? Was it possible that what Marcus had said was true?

"I've come to take you home." She kept her voice steady. After all, she was the levelheaded one in the family.

"Home?" He looked so hopeful, and so abashed. "I can go home now?"

"Yes." She held out her hand. "We'll go home. Together."

"Together." His face lit up in a thousand-watt smile. "Damn. It's good to see you."

"Is it ever," Oggie muttered. "Where the hell have you been, gal? Never mind, you're here now. Take him home. Please."

Everyone joined in.

"Yeah, get him outta here!"

"We heard enough!"

"He's been jabberin' for hours!"

They stomped and applauded.

Patrick flourished his whiskey bottle and bowed to one and all. "What a woman, huh?"

"Yeah, she's one of a kind," some chivalrous fellow concurred.

"Now get off the damn table!" Jared commanded.

"Okay, okay." Patrick tossed his bottle to Tim Brown, and bent to a crouch. Regina smiled at him, still holding out her hand.

But then his gaze shifted. He was looking past Regina. "Oh, no..." Slowly he straightened without leaping down.

Regina—and everyone else—turned to see what he saw.

It was Chloe. Behind her, the double doors were still swinging. And in her hand there was a small but deadly looking gun.

"Patrick!" Chloe shouted. "She can't have you, Patrick! I won't let her!" Jared started to leap the bar. Chloe spun and aimed her gun at him. "Don't try it." Jared froze.

Chloe swung the gun around again, this time toward Regina. "I'll get rid of her, Patrick. You'll see. You watch..."

Regina, disbelieving, couldn't move. She stood frozen to the spot. But Patrick, calling on the famous Jones reflexes once again, surged into action just in time.

He vaulted from the table. Regina gasped as he grabbed her shoulders and spun her around, putting himself between her and the woman with the gun.

"No, Patrick..." Regina tried to protest.

But she was too late. There was a loud, sharp *crack*.

Then Chloe's scream.

Regina and Patrick stared at each other.

"Patrick?" Regina whispered in stunned disbelief. "Patrick?"

Chloe shrieked, "Oh my God, no! Not Patrick! It wasn't supposed to be Patrick!"

Patrick smiled at his wife, a sweet and gentle smile. And then he slowly crumpled to the floor.

Chloe, sobbing and wailing uncontrollably, dropped the gun just as Jared reached her side and grabbed her.

Pandemonium ensued.

"He's shot!" It was Oggie's voice, bewildered and full of anguished wrath. "That crazy woman's shot my boy!"

Everyone was shouting.

"Call an ambulance!"

"Chloe Swan's shot Patrick Jones!"

"Somebody get the sheriff!"

Regina barely registered the uproar. Her whole attention was focused on the fallen man at her feet. Her knees seemed to bend of their own accord as she sank to her husband's side.

She noted the spreading pool of blood beneath him. She knew it would be dangerous to move him. But she *had* to touch him. Carefully she reached out a shaking hand to smooth his hair.

"You foolish man. You shouldn't have done that." She murmured the words very softly, sure he couldn't hear them.

But then her breath caught as his eyes opened and he granted her one of those rakish grins of his. "A decent wife is... damn near irreplaceable."

"Oh, Patrick..." She felt the first hot tear slide over the dam of her lower lid and trail down her cheek.

"Lighten up," he advised, squandering his fading strength to lift a hand and tenderly wipe the tears away. "Things could be worse...."

She clasped the hand that caressed her cheek, then brought it to her lips. "Shh. Don't talk. And please don't move. They're calling the ambulance. You're going to be all right, I promise you."

"Yeah. Sure. But in case I'm not—"

She touched his lips. They felt frighteningly cool. "Shh. Don't say that. Don't even think it." Someone handed her a coat, which she wadded up and placed beneath his head.

"Damn it. Stop fussing over me and listen."

"Oh, sweet Lord." She gave the makeshift pillow one more pat.

"Listen..."

"Yes. Yes, all right. What is it?"

"Help Marybeth take care of the girls."

"I will. You know I will."

"And..." He lifted a hand again, but this time only pawed the air weakly with it before letting it fall. He was panting. "Come closer. I can't..."

She bent nearer, so close she could feel his labored breath against her cheek. And he whispered with so much effort that it broke her heart to listen. "I love you, Gina. You're the best damn thing that ever happened to me...."

Regina swallowed a sob. He loved her, *loved* her. They were the words she'd never dreamed she'd hear from him. And yet she *was* hearing them.

She bit back the tears, wanting to be strong for him, right now, when he most needed her strength.

Yet still the hard truth assailed her.

She had thought herself above him, she could see that now. She had been so full of her own special brand of well-bred arrogance. She had seen herself as a prudent, genteel woman who had married beneath herself . . . for love.

Oh, Lord, what vanity.

She'd known nothing of love. *This* was love. This hellion lying in his own blood from the bullet he'd taken to save her, this incredible man who was willing to use the last breath in his body to tell her what was in his heart.

Regina opened her mouth to say what an utter fool she'd been. But then she closed it, because she realized that Patrick couldn't hear her anymore. With a gentle sigh, he had slipped from consciousness.

"Where's that damn ambulance?" Oggie, right beside her, wanted to know.

The old man had no sooner finished asking the question than they all heard the scream of the siren. The ambulance was on the way.

Chapter Seventeen

Not much more than a month later, in the little meadow at the crest of Sweetbriar Summit, Regina spread her blanket beneath the oak. Then she kicked off her shoes and went to the spring, where she drank the clear water from her cupped hands.

She returned to the blanket and sat down, breathing in the clean air, glancing up now and then at the fat white clouds that drifted by, thinking how the change of seasons was coming. The grass was already golden. The leaves of the oak, a black oak, were going brown.

But the day itself was warm, with a hint of a breeze. A perfect day for lovers. And this was the perfect place for a lovers' tryst. The timing, also, was just right. The girls were in school and wouldn't be home for hours.

Regina lay back on the blanket, a soft smile on her face. She closed her eyes, thinking that the last time she came here she had not known she was waiting until she heard the whisper of footsteps in the grass.

This time, of course, she knew. She knew she was waiting for a man. A certain man. The one man for her.

A peacefulness came over her as she lay there stretched out beneath the sky. She let her mind drift, like the white clouds above, in a state somewhere between sleep and waking.

Which was why she failed to hear the footsteps this time. She didn't even know he'd come, until he was standing above her, blocking out the sun. She opened her eyes, and brought a hand up to shade them.

"Patrick."

She could see that the hard climb up the side of the steep hill had tired him. His face was slightly pale. But she quelled the nursemaid within her. She'd been his nurse for a month now. Today she would be much more.

She gave him a welcoming smile and sat up. Then, lazily, she stretched.

He was holding a long strip of rather rumpled red tickets. He dropped them in her lap. She gave a low chuckle, picked them up and idly twisted them around a finger. She had left them, along with a brief note and the treasure map she'd saved from the first time they'd come here, on his pillow. The note had said:

> Keep going until you get to the top. Bring the tickets for old times' sake.

He crouched down beside her. And then he ran a finger along the line of her cheek.

She looked up from the tickets and into his eyes. Not breaking the hold of his gaze, she set the tickets aside.

Patrick leaned closer, so that his lips were a breath's distance from her own. And then he closed the distance.

Regina sighed and let her eyelids flutter closed as he kissed her. How long had she waited, dreamed of this moment? It seemed like years since she'd last felt his mouth upon her own in a kiss that promised all manner of delights.

Even after they'd dug the bullet out of him and said he would recover, she'd feared for him. And she'd had her share of nightmares in which she lost him forever and never knew the wonder of his loving touch again.

But now, at last, he was well enough to meet her on Sweetbriar Summit. And to kiss her in that special way that set her whole being aflame.

His lips brushed hers in a series of teasing, exploratory caresses.

And then he sat back.

Her eyes drifted open to meet his, which were gleaming with the same promise she'd felt in his kiss. His face was no longer the least bit pale, and she was glad for that. If anything, she noticed with a small stab of purely feminine satisfaction, he looked a bit flushed—in a very healthy kind of way.

His hand cupped her head. He smiled, and she felt the deft movement of his fingers as, one by one, he removed the pins that held up her hair. The brown strands tumbled to her shoulders. He stroked her hair, combing it with his fingers as he'd always liked to do.

When he spoke, his voice was low and soft as the wind.

"The last time we were here, I made you promise to marry me. Remember?"

"Oh, Patrick..." How she loved the tender way his hand smoothed her hair.

"Remember?"

"Oh. Yes. Yes, I do."

"But this time . . ."

"Yes?"

"This time I'm going to make you . . ."

"What?"

And right there, on Sweetbriar Summit, with the autumn sky and the pine-covered mountains as witness, Patrick Jones demanded, " . . . Say you love me."

She didn't hesitate. "I love you, Patrick."

His hand went still, and then dropped to his side. He marveled, "Damn. I like the sound of that."

"I've loved you for a long time," she confessed shyly.

He sat back a little and studied her, a puzzled expression on his face. "How long?"

"Since the morning after you married me."

He snorted. "No kidding?"

"No kidding."

"Why the hell didn't you say so?"

"I was a fool."

He said nothing, only watched her face.

"What are you thinking?" she dared to inquire.

"Only that you might have been a fool—but you damn sure weren't the *only* fool."

"What do you mean?"

"I mean that, looking back, it seems like I've loved *you* since the day after I moved in next door to you."

"No . . ."

"Yeah. Remember, I came to borrow that cup of sugar?"

Regina nodded. She remembered very well.

"You were wearing a robe that covered every inch of you, holding on to the neck of it like you thought I might rip it off you. Not that I blame you. I *wanted* to rip it off you."

"You didn't."

"I did. I loved you even then, though I guess I didn't know it. I hadn't felt anything really strong for a woman since..."

"Chloe?"

"Yeah. And the way things turned out with her, I was never going to let myself get in trouble like that again."

Regina spared a moment to think of Chloe. It was said around town that Chloe had seen the error of her ways. But contrition would not be enough to get Chloe off the hook. She would have to spend some time in prison for what she had done.

Patrick wasn't thinking of Chloe at all. He repeated, "I was never going to fall for a woman again."

"I understand."

"But then there you were. I'd known you all my life. You'd been there all the time, but somehow, I hadn't noticed you. Then my old man said, 'Go take a look at her.' And I did. And it was like... Hell, there's no explaining it. Except I found that what I wanted was right next door.

"I was relieved. And anxious. I wanted to grab you and shake you and make you see in me what I saw in you. I wanted to break Marcus Shelby in half with my bare hands, just for seeing you first. And I knew I had to be careful, wait for the right moment, or you'd run like hell from me."

"The day of the picnic..."

"Yeah, it was the moment, and I took it. I made you mine. But I didn't figure it out, what I was feeling, until the night I married you."

She gaped at him. "You knew you loved me *then?*"

He nodded.

"But if you knew you loved me on our wedding night, why didn't you say so when I asked you, the next morning?"

"Hell, Gina." He looked away, out over the town where the leaves on the trees were going gold and the new roof was almost finished on the community church.

She took his chin in her hand and made him look in her eyes. "Please, tell me. It's important that you tell me." She cast about for the right words. "We need to share our heart's secrets with each other, to tell each other the things that are hardest to say. It's part of trusting, to say the hard things." She teased, "And you yourself said how important trust is in a marriage."

He faked a confused expression. "I did? When?"

"You know very well when." She was not going to be put off. "Say it. Come on. Why didn't you tell me you loved me when I asked you about it?"

"Hell."

"Come on."

Haltingly, he began, "Gina, a man has his pride."

"And?"

"And . . . we had things we wanted from each other. It seemed like we'd made a good bargain. You got a husband and a family. I got a decent wife to help me raise the girls. When you asked me if I loved you that morning after we got married, it just...seemed like I'd be putting myself at a big disadvantage, to go bringing love into it, since I knew you didn't love me."

Regina was silent. Then, "I know exactly what you mean."

He looked doubtful. "Yeah, right."

"I do, honestly. I know because I felt exactly the same way. I held back from saying I loved you, because I thought that if you knew how much I cared, I'd become the needy one, wanting something from you that you could never give."

They stared at each other. Then he grinned. "Damn. So we were both fools, huh?"

"Yes. Prideful fools. And I am sorry, Patrick. About the way I let Chloe come between us. I never really doubted you, I swear. I knew you would never betray me. I was just so jealous. You had loved Chloe in the past. And even though you didn't love her anymore, she'd had what *I* wanted—your heart."

His smile was rueful. "Well, I hope you've got the picture now."

She answered steadily. "Yes, Patrick. I've got the picture now."

He tipped her face up. "Gina, I didn't even really know what loving was. Until you."

Regina had to swallow to force down the lump in her throat. "Oh, Patrick..."

His chestnut brows lifted. "Yeah?"

"I'm so sorry, for the awful things I said to you, for the unforgivable way I behaved."

"Yeah," he agreed. "You oughtta be sorry." A devilish gleam came into his eyes. "In fact, I think that right now you just better show me how sorry you are."

"Oh, Patrick..."

"Come on." His hands were on the buttons of her blouse. "Show me."

And she did.

And after their passion had faded to sighs, Regina told him about the baby that was growing within her.

He stared at her. "A baby? We're having a baby?"

"Yes."

"When?"

"In the spring. I'm only about six weeks along, but I'm sure. I can feel the changes. And I took two home tests. They both came out positive. She'll be born in May."

"How do you know it'll be a girl?"

"I just do. I feel it. We'll name her after my mother. Is that all right?"

"Yeah, Gina. It's all right." He pulled her closer and kissed her hair. "Damn. We've got it all." The words were husky with emotion.

Naked in the sun, Regina smiled. Patrick was right. They had a home, and the girls and a baby on the way.

But most important, they had each other. They shared a love sweet, untamed and true—a love more splendid than anything Regina had ever imagined in the very wildest of her virgin dreams.

* * * * *

Take 4 bestselling love stories FREE

Plus get a FREE surprise gift!

Special Limited-time Offer

Mail to Silhouette Reader Service™

P.O. Box 609
Fort Erie, Ontario
L2A 5X3

YES! Please send me 4 free Silhouette Special Edition® novels and my free surprise gift. Then send me 6 brand-new novels every month, which I will receive months before they appear in bookstores. Bill me at the low price of $3.21 each plus 25¢ delivery and GST*. That's the complete price and— compared to the cover prices of $3.99 each—quite a bargain! I understand that accepting the books and gift places me under no obligation ever to buy any books. I can always return a shipment and cancel at any time. Even if I never buy another book from Silhouette, the 4 free books and the surprise gift are mine to keep forever.

335 BPA AQS3

Name	(PLEASE PRINT)

Address	Apt. No.

City	Province	Postal Code

This offer is limited to one order per household and not valid to present Silhouette Special Edition® subscribers. *Terms and prices are subject to change without notice.
Canadian residents will be charged applicable provincial taxes and GST.

CSPE-694   ©1990 Harlequin Enterprises Limited

Silhouette

SPECIAL EDITION™

WHAT EVER HAPPENED TO...?

Have you been wondering when much-loved characters will finally get their own stories? Well, have we got a lineup for you! Silhouette Special Edition is proud to present a *Spin-off Spectacular!* Be sure to catch these exciting titles from some of your favorite authors:

HOMEWARD BOUND (July, SE #900) Mara Anvik is recalled to her old home for a dire mission—which reunites her with old flame Mark Toovak in *Sierra Rydell's* exciting spin-off to ON MIDDLE GROUND (SE #772).

BABY, COME BACK (August, SE #903) Erica Spindler returns with an emotional story about star-crossed lovers Hayes Bradford and Alice Dougherty, who are given a second chance for marriage in this follow-up to BABY MINE (SE #728).

THE WEDDING KNOT (August, SE #905) Pamela Toth's tie-in to WALK AWAY, JOE (SE #850) features a marriage of convenience that allows Daniel Sixkiller to finally adopt...and to find his perfect mate in determined Karen Whitworth!

A RIVER TO CROSS (September, SE #910) Shane Macklin and Tina Henderson shared a forbidden passion, which they can no longer deny in the latest tale from *Laurie Paige's* WILD RIVER series.

Don't miss these wonderful titles, only for our readers—
only from Silhouette Special Edition!

BABY'S CHOICE

Those mischievous matchmaking babies are back, as Marie Ferrarella's Baby's Choice series continues in August with MOTHER ON THE WING (SR #1026).

Frank Harrigan could hardly explain his sudden desire to fly to Seattle. Sure, an old friend had written to him out of the blue, but there was something else.... Then he spotted Donna McCollough, or rather, she fell right into his lap. And from that moment on, they were powerless to interfere with what angelic fate had lovingly ordained.

Continue to share in the wonder of life and love, as babies-in-waiting handpick the most perfect parents, only in

Silhouette
R O M A N C E™